DEVOTED TO THE SPANISH DUKE

SASHA COTTMAN

Join my VIP readers for your FREE book

Click on the link at the end of the EPILOGUE to join my VIP readers and receive your FREE copy of A Wild English Rose.

Also by Sasha Cottman

The Duke of Strathmore

Letter from a Rake print, audio, FREE EBOOK

An Unsuitable Match (ebook, print, and audio)

The Duke's Daughter (ebook, print, and audio)

A Scottish Duke for Christmas (ebook and print)

My Gentleman Spy (ebook, print, and audio)

Lord of Mischief (ebook, print, and audio)

The Ice Queen (ebook, print, and audio)

Two of a Kind (ebook, print, and audio)

Mistletoe and Kisses (ebook and print)

Regency Rockstars

Reid (ebook and print) FREE EBOOK

Owen (ebook and print)

Callum (ebook and print)

Kendal (ebook and print)

London Lords

Promised to the Swedish Prince (ebook and print)

An Italian Count for Christmas (ebook and print)

Devoted to the Spanish Duke (ebook and print)

Wedded to the Welsh Baron (ebook and print)

Rogues of the Road

Chapter One

N arros Palace, Spain
    September 1816

Lisandro de Aguirre, Duke of Tolosa, was not one for parties or balls. They were usually dull affairs put on purely for political purposes. He wouldn't even be here tonight if it weren't for the fact that this magnificent gathering at Palacio de Narros was to commemorate the marriage of King Ferdinand to the Infanta of Portugal, Maria Isabel.

The wedding itself had taken place in Madrid some two hundred and seventy miles away. Those who supported the king were keen to celebrate, while everyone else had clearly made the effort to attend the party in order to keep up appearances.

Lisandro was firmly one of the latter. He knew that if he didn't make an appearance, his absence would be noted. And with the king becoming more unpopular every day, his spies were everywhere, looking for possible dissenters. There were rumors of people being arrested and disappearing. A smart man did not tempt that sort of fate.

He finished the last of his wine and handed the glass to a passing servant. He turned back to face the dance floor, continuing his slow search of the room. Somewhere in this crowd tonight there had to be a buxom señora willing to share his bed.

Come now, ladies. Gift me with your smile.

The back of a long blue gown caught his eye and he paused. While it was not unusual to see a garment of such color in Spanish society, it was the style which took him by surprise. Almost every other woman there was dressed in the high fashion of the Spanish royal court; this particular female was most definitely not.

Someone draws her inspiration from the English and French. Bravo.

Keen to get a better look, he waited for the wearer of the gown to turn around. When she finally did, Lisandro was certain that his heart had stopped. For a moment or two he simply stared.

From the light brown tresses that carelessly kissed her pale cheeks to those intoxicating full lips, she was every inch a true Basque beauty.

Lisandro licked his lips.

Perfection.

A pair of warm coffee-colored eyes stared back. He smiled at her. The slow, deliberate blink she gave in return was all the encouragement he needed.

His plans for seducing one of the noble wives would have to wait. He must meet this young woman.

Quickly, but not too obviously, he made his way around to the other side of the dance floor, stopping every so often to make sure she was still standing where he had last seen her.

She was; he knew this because he caught her gaze every single time he halted in his progress.

Where have you been all my life? You are stunning.

He could only pray that this mystery woman wasn't going to turn out to be some distant relative his mother had forgotten to mention. Lisandro was certain he was somehow related to every noble family in this part of northern Spain.

She gave a quick look back over her shoulder as she turned and headed for a nearby archway. The invitation for him to follow was clear.

My wish is your command.

On the other side of the arch, a door led to a wide stone terrace. The moment he stepped outside Lisandro took a deep breath. The cool night air was a welcome respite from the heat and cigar smoke of the crowded ballroom.

Brightly burning fire-cages and torches lit the terrace, while down below beyond the edge of Zarautz Beach lay the inky black of the Cantabrian Sea.

The mysterious woman made her way toward the set of steps leading down the rocky seawall and onto the sand. Lisandro followed, keeping a respectable distance.

A perfect, private interlude on the beach? What an excellent idea.

She reached the top of the stairs and stopped. *Blast.* He slowed his steps. She turned and faced him.

In the light from the flickering flames of a nearby torch, he caught the unmistakable look of uncertainty on her face.

Damn. She is an innocent playing at a game for grown-ups.

Lisandro had rules about young, sexually inexperienced women. Unless a man had in mind to marry the girl in question, they were strictly off-limits. Perhaps he would toy a little with her, rewarding her boldness, but go no further.

Finally, he reached her side and dipped into a low bow.

She gave him a soft but clearly practiced smile. Lisandro stifled a grin. Someone had trained her well in the art of the subtle flirt. Of showing a hint of interest but nothing more. Women kept their reputations carefully guarded in this part of the world.

"Buenas tardes, señorita," he said.

"Is it? I am not so certain. Considering that you, a perfect stranger, have been staring at me for the past while and have now followed me outside away from the other guests, I do have to question whether you are sincere in wishing me a good evening. Or is that just your usual opening line for women?" she replied.

Oh yes, you have been well taught. Under other circumstances, you and I could have a spot of delightful fun. Such a pity.

He chanced a look at her hands, grateful that the weather made it too hot to wear formal gloves. A white fan was held fast to her wrist with a piece of matching ribbon. Around her neck was a thick gold chain upon which hung a Santiago medallion. On her long, slim fingers there was no sign of a wedding or betrothal ring.

An unmarried beauty.

Whoever this vision of loveliness was, it seemed no one had yet laid claim to her. *Interesting.*

"You have me all wrong. I wish nothing but the best for you," he replied.

She looked him up and down, the soft smile on her lips informing him that she was pleased with what she saw.

"Are you enjoying this evening?" he asked.

She shrugged. "It is as I expected. A party full of people discussing politics and gossiping about one another. Most people are just here to be seen."

Lisandro raised an eyebrow at her words. It was unusual to find a young woman of quality who didn't enjoy major social events. It spoke of a mind that found interest in more substantial matters. "I thought all the young señoritas would be excited about this evening. It is not every day that the king takes a new bride," he said.

Her eyes narrowed. Her easygoing demeanor changing to one of guarded wariness. He was probing, seeking to discover what she really thought of the king. Did she see him as a tyrant too?

"Well, of course I was excited about tonight. All loyal subjects wish happiness for His Catholic Majesty. But the rooms of Narros Palace are stifling and crowded. That was all I meant," she replied.

Wise words. Never let anyone know what you truly think of the king unless you fully support him.

Lisandro came and stood beside the young woman; his gaze focused on the night sea. At the edge of the water, he could make out the line of white foam from the waves. He loved the ocean—it was a pity that his family home at Tolosa was some sixteen miles inland and these days, he rarely made the journey north to the coastal town of Zarautz.

"Don't you just love the smell of sea salt in the air?" she asked.

Lisandro chuckled. This girl was truly unlike most other women he had met. She was, like the air, a refreshing change. *Beautiful, intelligent, and interesting. What an enticing combination.*

"I must admit, I do find the ocean breeze does wonders for my soul. When I am out sailing in the deep blue, I find it exhilarating," he replied.

"Have you travelled far from Spain?" she asked, interest evident in her voice.

He turned to face her. "Yes. Many times. I have ventured as far north as Denmark, but my travels have mostly taken me to England and occasionally France."

She glanced at him. "I would love to see another land. To experience different people and their cultures."

"Well, I hope you do. Some of my closest friends live in England, and I would never have met them if I hadn't travelled," he replied.

He received a soft smile in return for his words of encouragement. A spark lit in his brain. There was a kindness about her, a warmth that had Lisandro suddenly imagining himself wrapping her up in his arms and taking her home—to meet his mother.

Who are you? I must get to know you better.

Heavy footsteps sounded on the stone paving behind them. The woman stepped away from Lisandro. Her gaze fell on whomever was approaching and her smile instantly disappeared.

Lisandro turned and all sense of gaiety fled.

Storming toward them, hands balled tightly by his side, was Diego de Elizondo Garza, the son of his family's enemy.

Mierda. Can't you see I am trying to work my charms on this young woman?

"Don de Aguirre, if you don't step away from my sister, I will kill you," said Diego.

Sister? Oh no.

The young woman, her face a study in shock, looked from Diego to Lisandro.

"Lisandro de Aguirre? Duke of Tolosa?" she said.

Lisandro nodded. Before this unexpected interruption, he had been on the verge of making introductions. He pointed at Diego. "He is your brother, so that makes you . . ."

Those brown eyes which had held so much promise only a moment ago were solid granite when she met his gaze. "Maria de Elizondo Garza, daughter of the Duke of Villabona. I see I was gravely mistaken in thinking you were a polite and honorable gentleman wishing to make my acquaintance. How foolish of me."

Sorry, Mamá. There goes that chance of fulfilling your wish for bebés.

Taking a quick step back, Lisandro gave a curt bow. "My apologies, I should have told you who I was sooner." He turned on his heel and walked away. The last thing he wanted to do was to cause a scandal. Attempting to seek favor with the unwed daughter of his family's worst enemy would certainly do that.

But Diego de Elizondo blocked his way back into the gathering. When Lisandro took one step to the side, intending to go around him, the young noble, his face set hard, mirrored his move.

Don't do anything foolish Lisandro. You were talking to his sister; let him have his moment of indignation.

Diego was a good seven inches shorter than Lisandro, who stood at six-foot-four-inches in height. And while he may have only come up to Lisandro's shoulder, he clearly made up for his lack of stature in temper. He stepped closer to Lisandro and pushed hard against his chest.

"What the devil were you doing near my sister?" he demanded.

"Nothing. I merely spoke to her. Believe me, if I had known who she was, I would not have done so," replied Lisandro.

Anger flashed in Diego's eyes, and he launched himself at Lisandro a second time. Lisandro took a deft step back, which had his attacker staggering as he touched only thin air. Lisandro determinedly held his composure.

Hot-headed fool. Why would you wish to start a fight at a royal wedding celebration?

Other guests began to file out from the palace, milling around the pair. Lisandro shook his head. Of course, people wanted to see a fight. The spectacle would give them plenty to talk about for the rest of the evening.

His gaze took in the quickly coalescing mob. He had seen this all too many times before and was not going to give anyone that sort of satisfaction—especially at his expense. *You people couldn't care less about either of our families. You just want to see blood spilt. Damn the lot of you.*

"Diego de Elizondo, I apologize for any offence I may have caused to you, your sister or your family." Lisandro spied a gap in the crowd and made his way toward it. Thankfully, Diego didn't attempt to follow.

Lisandro didn't want to fight anyone. He was more concerned with his bitter disappointment at discovering that the woman who had captured his attention tonight was someone he could never befriend, let alone form a relationship.

The only thing worse than being forced to attend a dull party was having made a fool of himself while trying to win over the daughter of his enemy.

~

As soon as the Duke of Tolosa had disappeared, Maria and Diego locked gazes.

Here we go.

She gritted her teeth, remaining silent while the other guests wandered back to the party. There was more than one grumble of disappointment about the lack of a brawl.

Her brother was furious. And since Lisandro de Aguirre had not given him the satisfaction of a public row, there was every chance that she would be next in Diego's line of fire.

He didn't disappoint.

"Why were you here on the terrace alone?"

"I wanted some fresh air. And to get away from the gossip. I have heard enough whispers of dissent about the king tonight to know that this is a dangerous place," she replied.

"Yes, there are too many people here being indiscreet with their words. But coming out here without a chaperone was also a foolish thing to do. You cannot be seen speaking to Don de Aguirre. How do you think that will look to Count Delgado?" he asked.

Maria bit back a sharp retort. It seemed that everything she did lately was viewed through the lens of what Count Juan Delgado Grandes would think and the impact her actions might have on her bride price. The sooner the betrothal negotiations between her father and Don Delgado were concluded, the better.

"I didn't know who he was until you arrived. But before then he was polite, and we engaged in a pleasant conversation. The instant I discovered his identity, I made my position regarding him quite clear," she replied.

"You must have known who he was!"

Maria shook her head. Until tonight, her only knowledge of the Duke of Tolosa was what she had been told by her parents and brother. "I have never met the man before. Other than not giving me his name, he didn't actually do anything wrong. He even apologized for that oversight."

Diego huffed. "Everything he did in coming near you was wrong. Maria, he is the enemy of our family!"

How many times had she heard the story of the century-old feud between the Aguirre and Elizondo clans? Maria was sure she could recite the whole thing word for word without pausing.

From the time she was able to understand, it had been instilled in her that the Duke of Tolosa was evil. In fact, anyone from the town of Tolosa was considered bad; even the priests were viewed with suspicion.

"I am well aware that Don de Aguirre is the devil incarnate. Should I have struck him with my fan? Would that have made you feel better?"

"Yes. You should have slapped his face with it," replied Diego. A curt nod finally had Maria sighing with relief.

Diego. Always looking for a fight. "I am not in the habit of assaulting strange men who have done nothing more than make pleasant conversation," she said.

Diego gave a tut of disapproval before offering Maria his arm. "Well, now that I have made my position clear, I think it best that you and I go back inside. We don't want you catching a chill out here. And Padre will want you looking well-rested and fresh for tomorrow."

It took all Maria's strength not to roll her eyes. "Yes, of course. One wouldn't want the meat looking anything but the most palatable for Don Delgado."

Her brother had the good sense not to reply.

As they wandered back into the party, Maria had a sudden thirst for a large glass of Malaga—anything that would take her mind away from her encounter with Lisandro de Aguirre.

The instant she had set eyes on him, her whole body had reacted. As the lofty noble had made his way across the room toward her, Maria's mouth had gone dry.

Right up to the moment he had given her his name she had been studying him with pleasured interest. He had experienced life outside the cloistered domain of Spanish nobility. He had seen something of the world. He had lived a life. Not to mention he was devilishly handsome.

Standing alone with him on the terrace, she had been captivated. His shoulder-length, dark hair, lightly oiled and swept back from his face, set her heart racing. And those lips, full of the promise of sensual kisses—she could just imagine what they would feel like on her skin.

Maria swallowed deep. Lisandro was no longer in sight, yet he still affected her whole being. Perhaps it was just because he would remain forever out of her reach that he was able to hold her interest. The aching hunger that had lingered long after he'd gone was surely only because she couldn't have him.

Forbidden fruit.

Her mother had always said she was too passionate, unable to control her wicked nature. That someday it would cost her a great deal.

She caught the eye of a passing servant bearing a tray of drinks and beckoned him over. After selecting a glass of the sweet Spanish wine, Maria raised it to her lips, silently toasting her lack of fortune when it came to men.

But no matter how hard she tried; her thoughts continued to return to the Duke of Tolosa. The tall, dark and illicit Lisandro de Aguirre.

She itched to run the back of her hand along his sexy stubbled face, then trace a soft line over the exquisite dimple on his chin. Maria shivered at the prospect of being *that* close to him.

A soft chuckle escaped her lips. She would never get the opportunity to do any of those things. There was every chance that she wouldn't ever set eyes on the Duke of Tolosa again. And if that wasn't a crying shame, Maria de Elizondo Garza didn't know what one was.

Chapter Two

The following morning, Maria was seated at a small balcony table in the villa her family had hired. Her home was thirteen miles away —too far to travel in one day for a night of wedding celebrations.

While finishing the last of her breakfast, she gazed lazily out over the Cantabrian Sea. Various fishing boats bobbed up and down on the dark blue waves while gulls cried overhead. It was the perfect coastal picture.

The only thing spoiling the moment was the presence of her brother, Diego, and his continued griping over the events of the previous evening. Maria had long given up staring daggers at him, but still held out some hope that he might take the hint and shut up about the Duke of Tolosa.

"The nerve of that man. He must have known who you were. I should have called him out and demanded satisfaction."

Maria took a long, deep sip of her hot *café con leche*, she hoped that soon the coffee would be enough to take her mind off her brother's insistent complaining.

Unfortunately, it wasn't.

"You can't fight a duel; the Pope has forbidden them. And it was a wedding celebration, so I hardly think King Ferdinand would have taken kindly to the knowledge that someone might have died on his happy day," she replied.

It wasn't as if her brother had ever found himself in the position where he had to use a sword or pistol against a man. The worst adversary Maria hoped he would ever have to deal with was an Iberian wolf or a brown bear.

Her gaze returned to the sea. The tide was slowly working its way out, and several boats were making their way into shore. Maria doubted she would be able to enjoy lazy mornings like this once she was wed to the ambitious Juan Delgado.

She reached for her gold chain, silently chiding herself for having forgotten to put it on this morning. As soon as she was finished breakfast she would go and get it. Maria never went anywhere without her Santiago medallion.

"And speaking of happy days, how are the dowry negotiations going this morning? Father did not seem pleased when I saw him earlier," she added.

"Not good. Juan Delgado is a tough negotiator. After everything Papá has offered him, he still asks for more. At the rate things are going, you will be lucky to be a bride before Christmas," replied Diego.

What a shame.

She would have to remember to feign disappointment in front of her father if he could not seal the agreement today.

A shadow fell over the two siblings, and Maria glanced up to see her father's trusted advisor, Señor Perez, standing close by. The grayhaired man smiled and bowed to them. "Don Diego. Doña Maria. What a beautiful morning. The sun is shining and there is not a cloud in the sky. God is truly smiling down upon us today."

Maria and Diego exchanged a grin. Señor Perez was always one for waxing lyrically.

Diego rose from his chair and politely bowed to Maria. "I must go and see how things are progressing. Though I don't hold out much hope."

Señor Perez nodded. "Good luck. They were still haggling over jewelry when I left a few moments ago."

Maria finished the last of her coffee and also rose. Señor Perez held out his arms to her, offering a hug. "Don't worry. Your father will eventually get things settled. In the meantime, would you like to go for a walk along the beach? One of the villa staff mentioned that the fishermen often have delicious, fresh clams for sale."

She had known this man all her life, considered him as an uncle. Spending a warm summer's morning with him strolling along the sand was a perfect idea. The cool sea breeze would help to clear her mind.

"Let me go and get my necklace and then I shall meet you at the stone steps which lead down to the beach," she said.

"How about we leave now? The fishermen may be gone by the time you return if we delay. And it would be such a pity to miss out on those clams. I promise we won't be gone long," he replied.

She nodded. "Alright, let's go. I am sure I can survive for a few minutes without my pendant."

A short while later Maria followed Señor Perez as he led her onto the golden expanse of Zarautz Beach. She took in a deep breath; the salt air was magnificent. Being this close to the sea always did something to her mood.

Lisandro de Aguirre was right about the lure of the sea.

Not wishing to ponder why her thoughts kept returning to the Duke of Tolosa, Maria took hold of Señor Perez's arm and grinned up at him. A change in topic was in order.

"I didn't see you at the ball last night," she said.

He screwed up his face. "You know me—I am never one for those sorts of things. All that dancing and making polite talk? No, thank you."

"Oh, come now, *tío*, I have seen you dance. The ladies are always eager to take a turn of the floor with you," replied Maria.

He leaned in close and met her gaze. The pale color of his face and dark circles under his eyes gave her pause. He looked tired. "I took to my bed early last evening. I am not a young man anymore. I need my sleep."

The sound of men crying 'heave' came on the wind, and Maria turned to see a fishing boat being dragged into shore. Pots, nets, and rope were tossed over the side. Señor Perez gently nudged her.

"Let's go and see if they have any clams for sale. I would love some tossed in garlic."

Maria lifted her skirts, doing her best to keep them dry. The thought of fresh seafood was a nice distraction to her new concerns about the health of her father's trusted servant.

As they drew closer to the small boat, the fishermen stopped their work and stood with heads bowed. One by one, they slipped off their woolen caps, acknowledging Maria.

"*Buenos días,* good gentlemen. Did you have a successful fishing trip?" said Señor Perez.

The men looked from one to another, then finally, one of them stepped forward and bowed low. "We caught many fish," he replied.

Maria released her hand from her friend's arm and moved toward the boat. She was keen to see what was in the fishing pots. "Do you have any clams, or should we ask farther up the beach?"

The man gave a cheery grin, then nodded. "Yes. Yes, we have clams. Come. Come see."

He motioned for her to come closer to the boat, but the water made her hesitate. Wet skirts would surely earn her a scolding from her mother.

"Bring the pots over onto the sand," said Señor Perez. Putting his hand into his jacket pocket, he withdrew a handful of coins. The money quickly had the desired effect, and two large pots were lifted over the side of the boat and carried to where Maria and he stood.

Several more of the fishermen now came ashore, but two remained with the boat. They began to drag it back out into the water.

Maria leaned over the first of the pots. "These look good. They—"

Strong arms wrapped about her waist. She was jerked violently off her feet.

"What are you doing? Unhand me this instant!" She kicked and squirmed, fighting for release. But the man who held her only tightened his grip. With her arms pinned hard against her body, she struggled to make any headway against her captor.

"Señor Perez help me!" she cried.

Her friend stepped forward his hand raised. "Please no!" he pleaded.

A large black cudgel quickly silenced him. He collapsed onto the sand, unconscious.

Maria screamed.

The wind swiftly carried her protests away. Then a huge, rough hand came over her mouth, ending any further chance she had to cry for help.

Her abductor was strong, her continued efforts to gain release achieving nothing more than to tire herself. From out of the group of fishermen, another man appeared. She whimpered at the sight of his badly scarred face. From the way he spoke, it was obvious Spanish was not his first language. Maria caught snippets of words which she knew to be English.

In his hands he held a large brown hessian sack. As he lifted it up and placed it over her head, all her hope fled.

"Get her in the bloody boat!" he bellowed.

Maria fought one last desperate time, lashing out with her feet. Her boot connected with a body, and a cry of pain was her reward.

She didn't get another chance to strike as a sudden sharp jolt of agony tore through her brain. Her world spun sickeningly, and she knew no more.

Chapter Three

*T*wo *weeks later*
      Castle Tolosa, Spain

At the top of the ridge, Lisandro pulled back on the reins of his gray
Barb and the horse slowed to a gentle walk. It was mid-morning on
another fine day at his family's estate.

In the field below him, his workers were busy preparing the soil for
the new wheat crop which would be planted at month's end. The
strains of an old Spanish folk song drifted to his ears and he smiled.
Somewhere down there was his leading hand, Manuel, happily entertaining everyone while they worked.

The horse came to a stop, and Lisandro sat back in the saddle,
lifting his face to the sun. "*La bendición de Dios,*" he whispered. This
truly was a country blessed by God.

Spain was at peace. The war with France over. The only gray clouds
on his horizon were the rumblings of discontent over the return of
King Ferdinand. Lisandro privately hoped his country would not come
to civil war, but the king was proving himself the worst of monarchs.

But for the time being, Lisandro was home and working to make the Tolosa estate financially strong once more. He had neglected things while away at war. Put his own life on hold while fighting to free his country of the influence of Napoleon.

Time at home had him thinking about many things, especially his future.

He was lonely. His bed was empty. Lisandro ached for someone whom he could share his life with and raise a family. A special woman to hold his heart. A wife.

Finding the right woman was proving more difficult than he had expected.

Such a pity that the beauty at that ball was Maria de Elizondo Garza. If she were anyone else, she would have been perfect.

A small cloud of dust on the road caught his eye, stirring him from his thoughts. Lisandro scowled. Few travelers ventured off the main thoroughfare, which ran through the old town of Tolosa on its way to the coast. This was a sleepy part of the world.

From his saddlebag, Lisandro produced a spyglass and trained it on the moving dust. It was a carriage, headed at speed toward Castle Tolosa. He couldn't quite make out the markings on the side; they appeared to be covered with black cloth.

Odd.

He gritted his teeth. In his experience, unexpected visitors rarely brought good news. And this guest clearly did not wish to announce his or her arrival.

Tucking the glass back into its bag, Lisandro turned his horse's head and made for home.

In the courtyard of the castle, he came upon the coach. After dismounting from his horse, he handed the reins to a servant and walked over to inspect the carriage. He lifted the black cloth which covered the door, frowning at the sight which met his gaze.

A black and white checkerboard shield, topped with a silver helmet and crest of feathers, was emblazoned on the side of the carriage. The Elizondo family coat of arms.

He swore under his breath. What the devil was his family's avowed enemy doing at his home?

"Don de Aguirre?"

Lisandro turned, and flinched. Diego de Elizondo was standing in front of him. Instead of waving his fists threateningly in Lisandro's face, Diego bent himself in a deep bow. There was no sign of a sword or a pistol on his person. *What on earth is going on?*

The hairs on the back of Lisandro's neck rose. Suspicion tingled throughout his body. Why would an apparently unarmed Diego be here? He feared to know the answer.

Remember who you are, Lisandro de Aguirre. This man is a guest; treat him with the courtesy that deserves. If he causes any problems, then you will be well within your rights to kill him.

He grimaced at the thought; Lisandro hoped that his days of bloodletting were well behind him.

"Don Diego, this is most unexpected. Have you perhaps lost your way?" he asked, attempting a touch of levity.

The instant that Diego finally righted himself and met Lisandro's gaze, all thoughts of humor disappeared from his mind. The heir to the title of Duke of Villabona was a younger man than himself, but in the weeks since Lisandro had last set eyes on him, Diego appeared to have aged, a good ten years.

"I come in peace to seek your guidance and help. Could we perhaps speak somewhere in private, Don de Aguirre? I have a grave matter to discuss," replied Diego.

Lisandro patted his coat pocket, pleased that he had not given up the habit of carrying a loaded pistol with him at all times. Confident that he could defend himself if necessary, he dismissed the gathered servants.

He caught the eye of one of his most senior estate staff and the man nodded. If anything did happen to Lisandro, Diego wouldn't be leaving Castle Tolosa alive.

Contingencies in place, he led Diego out around the side of the castle through a stone archway and into a small but high-walled garden.

In the center of the garden was a wooden gazebo, its roof formed by ornamental grape vines. This was his mother's personal place to come and sit when she wished to escape the heat of the day during the height of summer.

Lush green English ivy trailed up the walls, covering almost every inch. While the effect was visually stunning, it also served a purpose. The glossy leaves provided a perfect form of sound insulation. Nothing echoed in the enclosed space.

He motioned toward the table and chairs which sat under the gazebo, but Diego shook his head. Instead, he reached into his coat pocket.

Lisandro stiffened.

Don't be a fool, Diego.

He sighed with undisguised relief as Diego pulled out a piece of paper and handed it to him.

~

Don Antonio de Elizondo. Duke of Villabona,

Maria is as yet unharmed—but this could change. She is far from here, so do not seek to rescue her.

The sum of 250,000 Spanish Dollars is to be handed to the head priest at Santiago Cathedral in Bilbao.

Once we know the ransom has been paid you will receive further instructions.

~

Lisandro read the note a second time.

All the saints in heaven.

He had dealt with enough of these sorts of situations to know that the people who had taken Maria were professionals. Only amateurs added threats of bodily harm to ransom notes. It was awful to think that the beauty from the wedding ball had been kidnapped. But he wasn't sure as to what it had to do with him.

Odd that the kidnappers stated the ransom amount in dollars not pesos. Only foreigners call our currency Spanish dollars. Perhaps that's a clue as to who could have taken Maria.

When he lifted his gaze from the paper, he asked the question which had been forefront of his mind from the second he saw the Elizondo family coach. "Why are you here?"

Diego pointed to the note. "Because my father has done every-thing, he can to find Maria. Even Don Delgado has combed the country far and wide. There is no sign of her."

"Don Delgado? What does the Count of Bera have to do with this?" replied Lisandro.

"He and my sister are meant to be betrothed shortly."

Lisandro kept his opinion of Don Delgado to himself. Now was not the time to make mention of his lack of regard for the count. At least the man had done what he could to find Maria.

"Don de Aguirre, I am here because while our families are sworn enemies, I believe you are the only man in Spain who stands any real chance of finding my sister alive and returning her to us," he added.

Diego's words set Lisandro's nerves on edge. What exactly did he know about Lisandro's past that would have allowed him to form that sort of opinion?

"I am but a simple wheat farmer," Lisandro replied, keeping his voice steady.

Diego, to his credit, met and held Lisandro's gaze. "But you were more than that when you helped force the French to release the king from imprisonment. I have heard a whisper that you worked with the English during the war. Do I need to go on?" asked Diego.

It was common knowledge that Lisandro had been personally thanked by King Ferdinand for his efforts in returning him to the Spanish throne. But Lisandro's clandestine dealings with the British were not something he was keen to make public.

He held up his hand. "Enough. Let us agree that I have a history of dealing with difficult situations and leave it at that, though I do find it somewhat strange that you are the one who has come to me for help rather than your father. From the way you have disguised your family coat of arms on the travel coach, I take it that the Duke of Villabona doesn't know you are here."

Diego looked back toward the entrance of the garden before turning and stepping in close. "I fear that someone in my father's house is involved in Maria's disappearance. And they must have been working with someone in Zarautz in order to coordinate the kidnap-ping of my sister. I don't know who or how, but I feel it in my bones. A loyal family advisor, Señor Perez, was attacked when my sister was taken, and that also gives me great cause for concern. The man was found dazed and wandering the beach several hours after Maria disappeared. If whoever is behind this outrage is prepared to attack an honorable old man such as him, who knows what else they will do to my family? I think it imprudent to involve my father at this juncture. Too many eyes are watching him."

"Then why not pay the money? While what they are asking for is a king's ransom, the kidnappers must know that your father will be able to find it," replied Lisandro.

"If only it was that simple. This is not the first ransom note we have received. An earlier amount was already paid. When we delivered it to the head priest at the cathedral in Bilbao, instead of handing over Maria, he gave us the second demand. The unfortunate man was most apologetic," said Diego. The young man tugged the hat from his head and raked his fingers through his hair. He closed his eyes and screwed up his face.

Lisandro doubted Diego could look any more uncomfortable. He must have swallowed a great deal of pride before deciding to come cap-in-hand to his enemy, asking for help.

"My father has fallen out of favor with the king. I have a horrible suspicion that powerful men are behind all this—men who don't care whether Maria is returned safely to us or not."

You, poor man. I cannot begin to imagine what you must be going through.

Pity for the son of his enemy filled Lisandro's heart. No one deserved to suffer the way Diego de Elizondo had.

"My father would beat me if he heard me say this— but Don de Aguirre, I think you are a man of honor. I am begging you to help save my sister."

Lisandro had dealt with kidnappers before; he even had friends who did it professionally in return for a hefty fee. But the tenuous state of his own finances wouldn't enable him to get very far if he had to pay his way in order to find Maria.

"I am not sure how much use I would be, considering the situation between our families," he replied.

"If you want money, name your price. I will pay whatever it takes to get Maria back," said Diego.

Lisandro scrubbed at his face with his hands. For some odd reason, the thought of taking money from his foe didn't quite sit right with him.

But this might be an opportunity to gain something else of greater value than just money. Perhaps even finally put an end to this ridiculous feud—and create a bond between us.

"You have been honest with me, Diego, so it is only right that I tell you my purse is almost threadbare, and I will need money to fund this mission. As to any other payment—I don't want your gold. My reward price, which is not negotiable, is that if I manage to rescue Maria, you allow me to attempt a friendship with her."

Diego frowned. "I don't understand."

How do I put this? Hmm.

"I found your sister to be both beautiful and enchanting; she and I made a small connection that night on the terrace at Palacio de Narros. A connection that I would like to see grow," replied Lisandro.

Realization appeared on the other man's face. He let out a low whistle. "That's a high price you ask of both my family and Maria."

If Lisandro did manage to find Maria and bring her home, there was every chance that at some point in the journey, the two of them would find themselves alone. A young unwed, Spanish noblewoman could easily lose her reputation if that ever came to light. A reputation which would only remain secure if she somehow found a way to marry her liberator.

Of course, if he put his mind to it, he could find ways to avoid being alone with her. But perhaps he wouldn't; and in doing so Lisandro could turn the situation to his advantage. Gain the opportunity to get to know Maria. And she to change her mind about him.

Say yes. Let her and I discover what could be possible between us.

"Diego, I promise I will do everything I can to find your sister. Whatever else comes after that, you have my solemn word that Maria will be given as much choice as possible," he said.

Diego nodded. He reached into his coat pocket and pulled out a gold chain. A religious medallion hung on the end of it.

Maria was wearing that the night of the ball.

"This is Maria's. She usually wears it but must have forgotten to take it with her when she went for that ill-fated walk on the beach. If you find her, give this to my sister. She will know who sent you."

Lisandro nodded. It made sense for him to have something to give to Maria to let her know that he was working on behalf of her family. Considering the long, dark history between the Aguirre and Elizondo clans, he could see how it would be hard for her to trust him without some form of proof that he was not in league with her kidnappers.

Lisandro beckoned toward the nearby gazebo. "Come, sit—tell me everything you know. However insignificant it may seem, do not leave out a single detail. It may mean the difference between getting Maria back or holding a rosary service for her."

Later that day, Lisandro sent Diego home in his unmarked coach with a solemn promise that he would do all he could. After accepting a bag of silver coins and bidding Maria's brother farewell, Lisandro went in search of his mother.

If he was about to go and rescue his potential future wife, the dowager Duchess of Tolosa should at least have fair warning.

Chapter Four

While Zarautz was the playground for the Spanish royal family and other nobles, it also had a dark underbelly. Lisandro knew all the immoral and foul places where the local criminals gathered. After taking a room at a quiet and respectable inn, he made for the less savory part of town.

For Maria to have been taken from the beach in broad daylight, the kidnappers must have had help from someone in Zarautz. Someone who knew the tides and also where she could possibly have been that morning. Locals would have had to be involved. And the longer Lisandro thought about it, the more Diego's words of worry about people close to the Elizondo family being complicit in Maria's disappearance made greater sense.

He didn't believe in happy coincidences; he had more faith in the power of a handful of coins. Those and a sharp sword were what usually got people talking.

Lisandro chose a grimy seaside tavern close to the villa where the Elizondo family had stayed during the wedding celebrations as the first place to scout for clues. As he walked into the inn, he dipped his functional hat toward the innkeeper, then settled himself at a table toward the back. His plain travelling attire of long black coat and dull brown trousers drew little attention from the other customers, which was exactly what Lisandro wanted.

Nursing a glass of brandy, he waited.

The patrons of the establishment slowly but surely got deeper into their drinks over the course of the night. The drunker they got, the louder and looser of lips they became.

He had just set his second gently nursed glass of golden heaven onto the table when a voice rose above all the others.

"You bloody Spanish are hopeless at handling your ships. How many times did your Armada try and invade merry old England? Too many times."

Lisandro searched for the loudmouth. There was a group of rowdy drinkers not far away. In their midst rose a man in a dirty red shirt. He climbed onto the table and held out his arms. It wasn't his clothing or behavior which caught Lisandro's attention—rather, it was his badly scarred face.

Someone at the Englishman's table swore at him in Spanish, and the rest of the gathering all laughed. The man clearly understood the jest. "*Hijos de perros,*" he replied.

His friends obviously didn't mind being told they were sons of dogs as they all lifted their glasses and toasted their companion.

The man reached into his coat pocket and proceeded to rain coins upon the heads of those seated at the table. A roar of approval and cheers rang out.

"Come on, drink up, my amigos. Lots of lovely Spanish dollars. There is plenty more where that came from!"

Lisandro froze. Why would a poorly dressed Englishman be throwing money around? Most sailors barely scraped by, so who was this scarred man?

And he talks of Spanish dollars, not pesos. Just like in the ransom note.

While he didn't believe in coincidences, Lisandro most certainly believed in good fortune. Zarautz was a sleepy fishing town; few ships from other areas docked there. Any sort of foreigner could seem out of place.

The noise level in the drunken group steadily grew louder. If Lisandro had not been such an experienced operative, he would have continued to watch the boisterous Brit, but over the next hour his attention slowly shifted and focused on another man seated at the table.

This reveler was well in his cups and had slowed his rate of drinking to the point where Lisandro reckoned on him lagging three glasses behind the rest of his friends. When the man shifted along the bench and struggled to his feet, Lisandro pulled his hat lower.

"*Buenas noches!*" the man cried.

"Go on, bugger off," replied the Englishman.

The man staggered to the front door and out into the street. The jeers and foul farewells of his friends followed in his wake.

It was a tense five-minute wait for Lisandro before he slowly rose from his seat. He pulled the collar of his coat up and turned his head away as he passed by the raucous group of drinkers and made for the exit.

Outside, he looked up and down the street, searching. Then his gaze landed on his prey. The staggering drunk was further up the lane, a short distance away.

There you are.

Following and interrogating drunks was never a fun task. They had a tendency to throw up when stopped and questioned, but they were always easy to track. An alcohol-addled mind made for slow going.

Lisandro caught up with the man a hundred yards on from the tavern and quickly pulled him into a nearby doorway. It was far enough away from the inn that anyone else leaving would not see them.

"My friend, you have had much to drink," said Lisandro.

The man grinned. "That I have, *señor*. Much wine. Much brandy."

"You sound like you have been celebrating. I hope it was good news."

The drunk leaned back against the inner wall of the building's entrance and stuffed his hands into his coat pocket. "A job well done, as my friend from Inglaterra would say. And a job that paid well."

He pulled a handful of coins out of his pocket, proudly showing them off. Several of the coins fell with a clatter onto the stone flagging.

A folded piece of paper fluttered behind them. Before the man had the chance to react, Lisandro bent and retrieved the items.

The coins were handed back; the paper was not.

"Do you think your friend might have some work for me? I could do with a spot of coin," said Lisandro.

The man shook his head. "You don't want to get involved with people like me—and especially not with Mister Wicker. Besides, this was a once-off. There is not a lot of call for kidnapping, even in my line of work."

"Oh, come now, my friend—there is always someone who needs to be kidnapped. Spain has lots of castles in which to hide a wayward prince or a noble daughter," said Lisandro with a laugh.

He got a low, dirty chuckle in response. "You are wrong. The farther away from home you can take them, the better. Only a fool would risk keeping a prize captive in Spain."

Lisandro froze.

When the ransom note had said Maria was far away, he had naturally assumed she was still somewhere in the country—possibly further south, closer to Madrid. Had he been wrong?

"Well, I had better be off. If I am late home again, my wife will make me sleep in the stables," said the man.

Lisandro reluctantly let the man go. Roughing him up would serve no purpose and it might put his accomplices on notice. Besides, he had no solid proof that these were the people who had taken Maria. At the moment he had only his instincts and a handful of small clues on which to go.

Yes, but what are the odds of some other noblewoman having been kidnapped?

This had to be fate. Diego's thoughts about a local connection possibly being involved made sense, as did his own growing suspicions about the scar-faced Englishman. All Lisandro's attention now focused on Mister Wicker.

Remaining hidden in the doorway, he retrieved the piece of paper he had quickly stuffed into his pocket and unfolded it.

Señor Alba and the special cargo sailed on the evening tide. Keep quiet about Plymouth and you will get the rest of your money when the ransom is paid. W.

"Oh Maria," he muttered. Maria de Elizondo Garza had been kidnapped and stolen away to England.

Lisandro screwed the paper up tightly in his hand and made a silent vow.

I will find you and I will bring you home.

Chapter Five

T he endless hours of darkness followed by rough, grasping hands forcing vile liquids down her throat had melded into one long nightmare for Maria. Where she was and with whom, she had no idea. The only thing of which she was certain, from the constant lull from side to side, was that she was onboard a ship.

"Drink."

It was one of a handful of words he ever spoke to her; the main form of communication favored by her abductor was rough manhandling. Her short intervals of consciousness usually consisted of Maria being dragged from her bed, head still covered by the sack. She was forced to drink, then use a bucket for her ablutions before she was shoved back onto the rough mattress where darkness would descend once more.

Her only source of comfort were the memories of her mother and the promise Maria had made in those rare, precious moments between long stretches of insensibility.

Mamá, I shall find my way home. We will be together again.

And then came the day when she woke to silence.

The bed no longer rocked, and the roar of waves was gone. Her hands and feet were still bound, but the coarse rope had been replaced by softer binds. Ones which did not burn her skin.

Unfortunately, her head, remained covered by the sack. Small pinpricks of light filtered through the small holes in the hessian.

At least I can finally see more than just darkness.

"Hello?" she whispered.

Her word, though muffled by the hessian, echoed in the quiet of the room. For the first time since she had been attacked on the beach, Maria sensed she was alone.

Tears pricked her eyes as she remembered those final moments. Of the cries of pain from Señor Perez and seeing him struck violently and falling to the ground. She sent a prayer to heaven, hoping against all hope that he may have survived the vicious assault.

She was still alive, and that was something to hold onto. Whoever had taken her clearly had plans.

If they wanted you dead, they would have killed you already.

The rattle of a key in a lock caught her attention. Footsteps accompanied the clink of chinaware and glasses. The soft *thud* of wood meeting wood had Maria guessing that a tray had been placed onto a nearby table.

Skirts shuffled toward her, followed by a disapproving 'tsk.' This was something different and unexpected. Her new jailer was definitely female.

Hands tugged at the sack over her head, lifting, pulling it free. Hope flared. Finally, she would be able to see again.

"Oh!" she cried as blinding daylight pierced her eyes.

Maria turned her head away, wincing as the overwhelming newness of sight assailed her senses. It took several minutes before she was able to focus properly. Only then did she attempt to look at the woman.

A plump matron dressed all in gray stood beside the bed. Hands on hips, she appeared totally nonplussed at Maria's behavior. "Now, the master says you need to be eating," she said. Her gaze ran over Maria's trussed up body, and she shook her head. "How the devil am I supposed to feed you? Honestly, anyone would think this lot had never staged a bloody kidnapping before."

Maria's English wasn't the best, but she understood enough. Any slim chance of her being able to plead for the woman to take pity on her and let her go died. This woman was clearly a willing member of the kidnap gang.

A second person entered the room—a man wearing a colorful mask. He looked for all the world like he had just stepped out of a ball or the famous carnival in Venice. If her situation hadn't been so dire, she might have found it amusing.

"*Ella ha comido?*" he asked.

She knew that cruel voice only too well. It had been with her all through the nightmare on the boat.

The woman huffed. "We are in England, so speak the bloody language. You know I only understand a few words of Spanish, and most of them are insults."

"Has she eaten?"

"No. I only just got here. I took the sack off her head and was still trying to decide how to feed her while she is trussed up like a chicken when you arrived."

With the mask on, it was impossible to decipher the man's response. He swore under his breath, then marched over to the bed. "I suppose untying you won't present too much of a problem. You can't get out, and even if you did, where would you go?"

He bent and rolled Maria over onto her side. Then, to her bone-deep relief, he loosened the knots on her bindings and removed them before pushing her back down. She lifted her hands and got her first glimpse of the damage caused to her wrists and arms by the tight ropes which had bound her for the long journey to England. Deep, black bruises and half-healed red wounds covered the lower part of her limbs.

"Thank you," she said.

He ignored her, then went back to berating the woman. "Get some fresh water and soft cloths. I expect Doña Maria will wish to bathe. After she is clean, then make sure she eats. And keep this door locked. Don't make me tell you that again."

Since her captor appeared to be in a charitable mood, Maria took a chance. "Please, *señor*, could you tell me how long I have been gone from home?"

"I don't know what sort of comfort this will give you, but you have been our captive for over two weeks. And in answer to what will no doubt be your next question . . . when your father pays the ransom."

He issued further curt instructions to the woman, then they both left the room. A key turned in the lock.

Two weeks. She was alone, held prisoner in a foreign country. Beyond help from anyone she knew. What were the chances of her ever seeing her family again?

The woman soon returned bearing a bowl of warm water, soap, and a cotton cloth. She allowed Maria a scant five minutes in which to wash and dry herself while she stood and watched.

"Here. Put this on." She handed Maria a plain beige woolen gown and a petticoat. The rough garments were nothing like her usual fine attire, but they were clean, warm, and functional.

After she had dressed, Maria was ushered over to a small table where a plate of something that resembled a Spanish stew sat. She took a mouthful and screwed up her face. *Esto es horrible*

Hunger forced her to eat a little more. The woman hovered nearby, watching Maria intently. She moved closer when Maria set down her spoon and pointed at the plate. "I want to see it empty," she said.

Maria blinked back tears, fighting against her growing fear; whoever had taken her knew what they were doing. They were determined and dangerous.

Her mind began to slowly whirl with all manner of questions. Who were these people, and why had they taken her? And what had happened to the brave Señor Perez? Was he even alive?

She had no answers. But what really mattered to her was the most pressing question of them all.

What would happen if her father didn't pay the ransom?

Chapter Six

T wo weeks later
London, England

Lisandro took the fastest possible ship and sailing route, but it was still almost a month since Maria had been taken before he finally arrived in London. He made straight for an address in Gracechurch Street and the only men in England he knew he could trust to help.

When the hack pulled up out the front of the coaching company office, he checked the address he had written on a piece of paper and frowned. The building was rundown, dirty, and didn't look at all like something owned by men of means.

His heart sank. Perhaps the time since the end of the war had not been kind to his friends after all.

He paid the fare and, grabbing his travel bag, climbed out of the carriage. His only consolation was knowing that the particular skills his friends had at their disposal were the kind that often didn't require money. While Lisandro had the silver coins which Diego had given him, he was not keen to start throwing money around in order to find Maria. Piles of easy cash tended to attract the wrong sort of people.

One sharp rap on the door of the coaching company went unanswered. So did the second. In frustration, he headed around to the rear mews. Hopefully someone worked in the stables.

The yard was little better than the front of the place. There were no coaches or staff, but there was a large pile of clean hay just inside the nearest stalls.

"What a sorry mess," he muttered.

A movement to his right caught his eye. A young boy, no older than six or seven, came strolling nonchalantly out of the stables. He stopped, took one look at Lisandro, then put his fingers to his lips and let out a loud, piercing whistle.

Footsteps rumbled. Lisandro looked up to the top of the building. Three figures appeared from out of an upper door and moved onto the landing. Pistols were pointed directly at him.

He didn't move an inch. These men were some of his dearest friends, but he also had no doubt that the weapons were loaded and cocked. There would be little comfort in having them apologize profusely over his corpse for having mistakenly shot him.

"I am Lisandro de Aguirre, Duke of Tolosa. I would appreciate it greatly if you gentlemen lowered your pistols," he said.

Two of the men instantly moved to disengage their weapons but the third kept his firmly aimed in Lisandro's direction. A wry grin sat on his lips. "How do we know it is you? Any poorly dressed Spaniard could turn up and claim he was the Duke of Tolosa."

Lisandro chuckled. "Well, I was me when I woke this morning and discovered, to my disgust, that I was back in the rat-infested stench-hole of London."

The final pistol was lowered.

Sir Stephen Moore hurried down the stairs to embrace him. Lisandro accepted the hug with good grace. For a man who dealt in blackmail and death, the Englishman was surprisingly effusive.

"The Duke of Tolosa. What brings you here?" he asked. As he asked the question, Stephen's gaze roamed over Lisandro's tatty coat and battered hat, taking it all in. True to form, it seemed he missed nothing.

"An important mission—one which means the difference between safely returning a young Spanish noblewoman to her family and having a very difficult conversation with them," he replied.

Stephen nodded. "Then you had better come inside." He turned to the boy. "Toby, go upstairs and arrange a pillow and blankets for Don de Aguirre. He will be staying with us."

The young boy screwed up his face. "What was his name?"

Lisandro beckoned the boy to come over. "I am the Duke of Tolosa. If I was English, you would call me Lord Tolosa, but because I am Spanish, I am Don Tolosa. Also, Don de Aguirre. But you may call me Lisandro if that makes it easier."

Toby might have been confused about the names and titles, but the lad was clearly not a fool. He dipped into a low, respectful bow. "May I take your bag, Lisandro?"

"No, I am happy to carry it myself. But if you know where I can get a strong cup of coffee, I would be forever in your debt, young Toby," replied Lisandro.

The boy scampered off in the direction of the nearby stairs and took them two at a time.

Lisandro waited until he had gotten to the top before turning to speak to Stephen. "I need to find the people who have taken this noblewoman, and quickly. To say I have little to go on is an understatement."

"Come upstairs and let's see what we can do."

If anyone in London was going to be able to help it was one of the gentlemen who had been pointing a gun at him only a few minutes ago. With a spark of relief in his heart, Lisandro followed Sir Stephen up to the offices of the RR Coaching Company—Rogues of the Road.

Inside, he was greeted by two of the others: Lord Harry Steele and Mister Augustus Trajan Jones. Lord Harry had a well-earned reputation for causing scandals in London high society, while Gus's career as a smuggler necessitated him keeping a lower profile.

"Where is the Duke of Monsale?" asked Lisandro. He needed as much help as he could possibly get in order to locate Maria's whereabouts.

"Monsale is at his country estate overseeing the planting of new crops," replied Harry.

Lisandro nodded. "I should be doing that too. The wheat was almost done by the time I left Tolosa, and hopefully they will be getting the barley field ready now. And what about George?"

"George is . . . well, let's just say he is keeping a low profile at present. A little thieving job went awry a month back, and he nearly got caught. It shook him up quite badly," said Gus.

When no one else added to the story, Lisandro let it go. The Honorable George Hawkins was a master thief. If he had come close to being nabbed during a robbery, it must have been a risky one.

Lisandro held out his hand to Harry. "And congratulations on your marriage; it was lovely to hear you had taken on a wife."

Harry grinned. "Thank you. Fatherhood is the next adventure looming in my future. Alice is with child."

"Well then, double congratulations," replied Lisandro.

After dropping his bag onto the long well-worn table which sat in the middle of the room, Lisandro searched inside it for his notebook. He took a seat as Toby appeared from another room, bearing a large cup. The boy set it in front of him, then bowed and stepped back.

"Thank you, Master Toby. You may go resume the task of mucking out the stables," said Stephen.

With the boy gone, they got to work. Lisandro explained the unexpected visit from Diego de Elizondo, and his own trip to Zarautz, as well as the conversation he'd had with the drunk in the doorway. He also showed them the note about the boat and made mention of the Englishman, Mister Wicker, who had been in the tavern.

At the end of it all, he sighed and reached for his rapidly cooling coffee.

"Bloody hell, that's a king's ransom. Though it is odd that they asked for a smaller amount at first and then didn't release Maria," said Harry.

Sir Stephen picked up the ransom note. "I am not that concerned about the money, but this Señor Alba is most definitely of interest. If he came to England with Maria, then he might well be our best chance at finding her."

Lisandro had gone down a similar road with his own thoughts, but he had reached a dead end. Having a name meant little in a bustling city of more than a million inhabitants.

A sly smile crept to Stephen's lips. "Lisandro, when was the last time you went to church?"

He frowned. What a foolish question. He was Spanish and a Catholic; he went every week. Even on board the ship bound for England, he had asked the captain to conduct a small Sunday morning service for the crew and himself.

His friend might be onto something.

Everyone in Spain goes to church on Sunday. And when you are not at home, you find a place to worship. Could it be that simple?

Rising from his chair, Lisandro met Stephen's gaze. Today was Saturday. Tomorrow, all of the major Catholic churches in London would be full of worshippers, including Saint James's church in Spanish Place. Any good Spaniard who happened to find himself in the English capital would be attending the Sunday morning mass.

From his time in London during the war, Lisandro had formed a close friendship with the parish priest, Father Hurtado. If anyone new had started attending Saint James's on a Sunday, Father Hurtado would know.

Lisandro pointed a finger in Stephen's direction and grinned. "I have a sudden desire to go and stretch my legs. All the way to the other side of Manchester Square, and St James's church. And there I may seek out a priest. Care to join me?"

Stephen smiled back. "I thought you'd never ask."

Chapter Seven

Lisandro and Stephen arrived early for Sunday mass the following morning. After their visit to St James's the previous day, they now had a plan in place. Every attempt to blend in with the rest of the parishioners had been made; both were dressed in regulation black suits with white linen shirts. Their morning coats did little however to hide their well-toned physiques and more than one young lady batted her eyelashes at them.

After taking their seats several rows back from the altar but to one side, they sat quietly, heads facing forward, and waited.

The aging Father Hurtado shuffled in, coming down to the front of the pulpit and stopping in front of one of the deacons. They exchanged a few words, after which the priest nodded his welcome to various parishioners as they made their way into the church and found a space in the pews.

Lisandro watched the Father's gaze as it swept over the gathering. When Father Hurtado put his hands together and held them to his lips, Stephen cleared his throat. "That's the signal."

The priest dropped his right hand and touched the front of his robe five times. With his left hand, he brushed away an invisible piece of lint eight times. As he turned and headed back toward the pulpit, his gaze locked with Lisandro's for the briefest of moments.

Right-hand side of the aisle, which makes our man on this side. Five rows back from the front. Eight seats in from the aisle.

Adrenaline coursed through him. Señor Alba was here in the church. The man who had helped kidnap Maria de Elizondo was sitting a matter of feet away.

He let out a shaky breath, knowing that while he would dearly have loved to step out and make his way over to where Señor Alba sat, seizing him violently by the throat, it wouldn't help Maria. If the kidnappers were any sort of professionals, they would have protocols set in place. If Alba didn't return from church, they may well have standing orders to kill their captive.

Stephen coughed. Then coughed again. Lisandro reached out and patted him gently on the back. "Are you alright?"

"I'm trying to find a reason for us to leave. A coughing fit seems as good as any," he replied.

The spluttering grew louder, and the people around them made not-so-subtle noises about the disturbance. With a dramatic shake of the head, Stephen pointed to the aisle and got to his feet. He and Lisandro beat a hasty retreat out the front door.

Outside in George Street, Stephen made a miraculous recovery. "What did you see as we left?" he asked.

Lisandro pulled a notebook out of his coat pocket and jotted down some pertinent details. Short, tidy moustache, and well dressed. Middle-aged, if the kiss of gray hairs at his temple was any indication.

"From the respectable gap between him and the next group of people in his pew, he appeared to be alone. I didn't get a long look at him, but he seemed comfortable in his skin. You wouldn't pick him as being a man who had stolen a young woman from her home," replied Lisandro.

"Damn. I was hoping we might get someone who looked furtive and out of place. The fact that he feels confident enough to risk venturing out into society tells us a great deal about the sort of people who have Maria," said Stephen.

For the next hour they stood on the opposite side of the street, waiting for Sunday mass to conclude. A little before midday, the first parishioners began to file out of St James's church. Lisandro took a step forward, intending to cross over and stand outside the church, but Stephen seized him by the arm. "Let me do this. I blend in better than you."

Lisandro narrowed his eyes at him. "What do you mean?"

"I mean, you look like a Spanish gentleman. If you start following him, he might try to engage you in conversation. Then the game will be up. If I tail him, all he will see if he checks behind him is another pasty-faced Englishman out for a Sunday stroll."

Lisandro nodded, annoyed with himself that Stephen seemed to have a stronger grip on managing things than he did. Lisandro wasn't one for playing second fiddle, but with so much at stake, his pride would simply have to endure it.

Stephen leaned in close. "Just remember you are the one who is going to have to get Maria de Elizondo home to her family. Springing her from her prison in London may be the easy part. Getting the two of you back to Spain is going to be fraught with danger."

Lisandro didn't even want to think about the journey home. All that mattered was finding Maria and then figuring out the best way to rescue her.

"Here we go," said Stephen.

His friend stepped nonchalantly off the pavement and crossed the road. He walked past the front of the church, then stopped a little way up the street to peer in a shop's window, a good ten yards behind Alba.

You are very good, my friend.

It was an honor to watch a master at work. For such a large man, Sir Stephen Moore possessed an almost magical ability to blend into crowds. People might see him, but he moved in such a way that their brains seemed to barely register his presence. He was a ghost walking among them.

The moment Señor Alba made to move away from the church and walk farther down George Street, Stephen followed. Lisandro waited until they were almost out of sight, then started slowly after them.

Ten minutes of turning left and right into laneways and streets kept him on his toes. More than once, Lisandro found himself leaping into a shop's doorway to avoid being seen. It was hard staying on both Señor Alba and Sir Stephen's tail without losing them.

He had just turned left out of Harley Street and into Queen Anne when a hand reached out and took a firm hold of his sleeve. Stephen pulled him into the front of a butcher's shop and dragged him toward the back. As he passed by the counter, Stephen nodded to the owner. "A pound of your best pork sausages please, my good man."

At the rear of the shop, he let go of Lisandro's arm. "Sorry. I had to do that. Couldn't have you wandering any farther down the street. Our friend just walked in the front door of number nine."

Relief washed over him. Finally, they had something solid to work with, to build their hopes upon. If they had located where Maria was being held, the chances of being able to successfully rescue her had suddenly risen.

The thud of the butcher's cleaver cutting through meat and then hitting the wooden block interrupted their conversation. Without batting an eyelid, Stephen pointed to a tray of pork pies which sat on the nearby counter. "Oh, and can we have a half dozen of the pies? They look good."

Lisandro wasn't the least bit interested in the pies; he wanted to know what they were going to do about Maria. He forced himself to take a slow, deep breath and calm down. This wasn't his first time dealing with a complicated situation. One couldn't just rush into action.

"We need to get around into the next street or the rear laneway and see what the back of the house looks like," he said.

"Yes. But first, we need to do some homework about the address itself. Who owns it, and who is currently living there? That information will give us options as to how we go about securing Maria's release. It may also provide vital information regarding the people behind her abduction. There are plenty of places in Spain, Portugal, or even France where they could have taken her. I still can't get my head around why they chose England," replied Stephen.

Lisandro had worked that question over and over in his mind. The fact that the kidnappers had taken Maria far away worried him greatly. Being the enemy of Don Elizondo meant he didn't have an insight into the Duke of Villabona's life or who, outside of his family, might hold a grudge against him. But one thing was universal—powerful men tended to make powerful enemies.

The butcher came around to the front of the counter, the meat wrapped in newspaper. Stephen dug into his pocket and pulled out some coins. He gave them to the man who counted out the required money, then handed the change back along with the parcel. They hurried out of the shop.

After crossing over Queen Anne Street, Stephen led Lisandro into a narrow laneway, then turned left. He stopped, ripped open the top of the butcher's paper, and pulled out a sausage.

"You are not going to eat raw meat, are you?" asked Lisandro.

Stephen raised an eyebrow. "No, but experience tells me that if they are any sort of self-respecting criminals, they will have a guard dog."

Lisandro grinned. Trust Stephen to be always thinking ahead.

At the rear of number nine, Lisandro bent and cupped his hands. Stephen placed his boot in the ready-made step and grabbed a hold of the fence with one hand while Lisandro lifted.

Lisandro groaned. His friend was no lightweight.

"You have been eating too many pork pies," he said, through gritted teeth.

"Stop complaining. Now hold still a moment," whispered Stephen.

Lisandro sucked in a breath and prayed that his knees would forgive him. A trickle of sweat slid down his back.

The low, threatening growl of a dog came from the yard, and he immediately fell silent. The last thing either of them wanted was for the animal to start barking.

Stephen whistled, then cooed softly. "Here, boy. I have a lovely sausage for you."

Crouched as he was, Lisandro couldn't see anything that was happening on the other side of the fence but snuffling and the wet sound of a sausage being gulped soon drifted to his ears.

"Good dog. Now you stay quiet and you will get another sausage."

A welcome tap on his shoulder had Lisandro lowering his hands,

DEVOTED TO THE SPANISH DUKE

and Stephen stepping away. Lisandro shook out his fingers as they walked back toward the street.

"You were right about the dog," he said.

"Of course, I was. Though it's only an old bulldog. From the way it swallowed those sausages down almost whole, I would say it is missing quite a few teeth. Oh, and it's only got three legs," replied Stephen.

That was good news. There was nothing worse than being chased by a beast in possession of a set of sharp teeth, especially when they were snapping at your heels.

On their way home, Stephen gave a full account of what he had seen in the rear of number nine while Lisandro made mental notes. By the time they had reached the offices of the RR Coaching Company, the kernel of a plan was already forming in Lisandro's mind.

A plan to rescue Maria.

Chapter Eight

I t was such a relief to be able to wash each day. The woman who kept the house for the kidnappers—Maria wasn't granted her name—boiled up a large kettle of water each morning and brought it upstairs. Fresh towels and soap were a godsend. Her captor had even begun to allow Maria a little more time in which to attend to her ablutions.

Her gratitude toward the woman didn't extend much beyond that, especially once Maria realized that the food she was being fed was laced with drugs.

With every meal came the same routine. Whatever was in her food rendered her unconscious within minutes of eating it. She would be given breakfast not long after the sun rose each day. The next thing she knew, Maria would wake in her bed, having no idea as to how she had gotten there. Through the window, she would see the pale light of early evening.

She'd have slept the day away.

But as the days rolled into one another; Maria began to sense that the woman was bored of the whole endeavor. She became inattentive and sloppy with her work.

In the beginning, she would remain in the room and wait for Maria to finish eating, but by the end of the first week she started leaving Maria on her own to eat, presumably only coming back once she had passed out.

The woman's disinterest created an opening—one which Maria did not hesitate to exploit.

On the morning of her fifteenth day in captivity at the house, she waited until the woman had once more left her alone with her breakfast. As soon as the door closed and the key turned in the lock, she picked up the knife from her breakfast tray and quickly headed over to the window. Pushing the curtains aside, she set to work on her secret project.

The window was opaque, which at first had been a disappointment as she couldn't see out, but it didn't take long for Maria to realize the benefits of no one being able to see her or what she was doing.

Over the past couple of days, she had managed to prize the bolt on the window latch loose, and this morning, her efforts were rewarded when it finally gave way.

"Ah," she gasped.

Success. Thank God.

Gently pushing on the frame, she cracked the window open an inch. She dared not go any farther lest someone outside notice. Placing her nose up to the gap, she took in a deep breath.

Delicious, fresh air filled her lungs, and joy sparked in her heart. It was a small step, but it gave her hope. She was determined to fulfil the promise she had made to her mother while onboard the ship.

Mamá I shall find my way home. We will be together again.

Hurrying back to her breakfast, which was the same standard offering every morning, a badly cooked pie, she cut off a large piece of it, then carried it over to the window. Crumbling it between her fingers, she let the wind take it away.

"It's a start," she whispered.

She would have to eat the rest of the foul pastry, but at least there was a chance now that she might be able to snatch a few hours of being conscious before the next meal—hours that could be used to figure out a way to escape.

Chapter Nine

They set a watch on the house. Each morning, Toby was taken over to Queen Anne Street where he would climb a tree in the rear of number seven and spend the day watching the comings and goings in the back garden next door. Just before leaving, Stephen would poke a sausage through the fence of number nine and have a friendly chat with the guard dog.

A flower cart vendor was given a few coins to relocate and set up across the road. The woman selling flowers was tasked with the job of noting who came and went via the front door.

By the end of the third day, Lisandro had a good idea of the routine of things. The woman who worked in the house was followed home one evening and afterwards kept under constant surveillance. Two other men also moved in and out of the house, but they appeared to be staying there.

A war council was summoned for the evening. In attendance were Stephen, Lord Harry, Gus, and Lisandro. Their chief spy, Toby, sat at the head of the table, a picture of seriousness.

"The old lady comes and sits on the steps about an hour after I arrive every morning. She smokes a cheroot right down, then goes back inside. I see her coming out again a few more times during the day, then she leaves just as the sun is going down," he explained.

Lisandro opened his notebook. "I confirmed again with the flower seller, and she informed me that the only person who uses the front door is Señor Alba. Which means later each day, we only have him and the two other unknown males in the house."

Establishing where the three men were during the night was one problem they were yet to address. Only a fool would go sneaking into a house not knowing where possible assailants could be lurking. Still, there was strength in numbers and if push came to shove, they could handle taking on the kidnappers. But they had to know where Maria was being kept. It wasn't unheard of for captives to be killed by their abductors rather than rescued.

Toby cleared his throat and glanced at Stephen. The handler of dirty deeds had taken the young orphan under his wing and was teaching him the tools of the trade.

"Go on, Toby. Remember what I have taught you. Even the smallest detail can be vital," said Stephen.

"Well, I was watching one of the upstairs windows early yesterday and I swore it opened just a crack after the old woman sat down on the steps to smoke. She was well away from it, so she didn't notice."

Lisandro sat forward, listening intently. Toby had a good eye for detail, and even in the short time that he had known the boy, Lisandro had come to trust his instincts. "Go on."

"Something fell out the window. I'm not sure what it was, but the dog raced over and quickly gobbled it up. Then he went back to his spot by the stables and lay down. I didn't see him move again for the rest of the day."

There was a sparkle in Toby's eyes, one which Lisandro recognized only too well—the joy that came from discovering a vital piece of information, something that could change everything.

"I had the spyglass ready this morning when the woman came out. Within a minute of her lighting her smoke, the same upstairs window opened. This time, I saw a small hand and what looked like a piece of pie. It was dropped just like yesterday, and again, the dog ate it."

"Did the dog sleep the day away?" asked Lisandro.

Toby nodded.

Gus let out a low whistle. Lisandro and Stephen exchanged a hopeful grin.

Someone hidden within the house was waiting until the house-keeper went outside to have her morning smoke and was then tossing food out the window. Food which, from the reaction of the dog, had clearly been drugged.

A small hand. A woman's, perhaps.

The memory of Diego de Elizondo as he stood in the grounds of Castle Tolosa and begged him to save Maria came clearly to Lisandro's mind. The heart-breaking look of desperation and fear on Diego's face would haunt him for all his days.

He sent a silent prayer across the many miles of sea to his home-land, hoping that Diego may somehow get his message.

I think we have found Maria.

The thought of Diego also brought back the rest of their conversation; and the reward Lisandro had asked to receive if he brought Maria safely home. To be allowed to spend time with her. For the Elizondo family to accept and acknowledge Spanish society's expectation that Lisandro would make Maria his wife.

And what if she doesn't take kindly to that idea?

Rescuing Maria from the clutches of a bloodthirsty band of kidnappers might well be the least of Lisandro's problems.

Chapter Ten

"This could all end rather badly," said Stephen.

Sir Stephen always said the same thing right at the start of any dangerous encounter. It was his peculiar way of saying 'take care and don't get killed' without actually having to give voice to his fears.

Lisandro checked his pistol for the fifth time, determined that he would not be the one on the wrong end of a gun. Glancing at his hands after he'd placed the weapon into its holster, he was relieved that they were steady and without any tremor. Cool heads were required for what lay in front of them tonight. Their lives, and the life of Maria de Elizondo Garza, depended on it.

The coach drew into the dark laneway at the rear of number nine Queen Anne Street and stopped. They waited in silence, ready for the signal.

When a loud rap came on the side of the coach, both men startled. Lisandro's pistol was immediately aimed toward the door.

It swung open and Augustus Jones appeared into the pale light. He looked to Stephen and then Lisandro. "Our men are in position across the road from the front of the house. As agreed, I will knock on the door while Harry and his men rush in from behind me."

He glanced at Lisandro's pistol and screwed up his face. "It goes without saying that I would rather not get shot by either of you two gentlemen this evening. So please take extra care if you decide to start firing."

Their plans didn't include having to shoot their way out of the house; the diversion at the front door would hopefully be enough for him and Stephen to be able to steal in and grab Maria. The sight of Stephen's powerful double-barreled flintlock did give him pause, but he knew the Englishman well enough to trust his instincts when it came to wielding weapons.

Lisandro pulled his pocket watch from his waistcoat and checked the time. It was almost eleven. Right on the hour, they would raid the house.

"Good luck. We shall rendezvous as soon as possible," said Stephen.

Gus closed the door and disappeared into the night.

Stephen leaned over and offered Lisandro his hand. "*Los santos te protegen*, my friend."

"Yes, and may the saints also protect you."

He followed Stephen out of the coach.

Earlier in the day, while the dog slept, Toby had climbed down from the tree next door and opened the gate to the rear yard. He had then closed it again and placed a stake in the ground in the laneway. From the house, the gate appeared to be shut fast, an illusion they all hoped would hold.

Reaching the break in the fence, Lisandro bent and withdrew the stake. The gate silently opened; they stepped inside.

The poor dog ambled slowly over to them and Stephen pulled out a sausage from his coat pocket. He handed it to the beast, who happily gulped it down.

"Off you go, lad," he whispered.

The bulldog wandered out the gate to where the driver of the getaway coach was waiting. He lifted the animal up into his arms and it happily settled on the seat next to him and went back to sleep. In the morning, the lucky dog would have a new home and all the sausages he could ever want.

Lisandro and Stephen hurried to the back door; a set of skeleton keys made short work of the lock. The door had just opened when a loud knock echoed in the front of the house. They quickly slipped inside and, after closing the door, hid themselves under the staircase.

"Yes, yes, wait a minute," grumbled Señor Alba.

He made his way downstairs, followed by another man. Lisandro turned to Stephen and held up two fingers.

Only one unaccounted for.

He caught the *click* of multiple pistols being cocked just before the front door was opened. Whoever was at the door was going to be met with force.

In an instant, Stephen had stepped out and fired his pistol twice. The two men dropped to the floor.

The next few minutes were a flurry of activity. Lisandro raced for the stairs with Stephen and Gus close on his heels.

A figure appeared at the top of the first landing, brandishing a rifle. In a deft move worthy of a flamenco dancer, Lisandro leaned to the left as Gus raised his pistol and fired at the man's head. The shot went wide and Gus swore.

Lisandro moved into position and aimed his pistol. The bullet found its mark and a patch of red appeared in the middle of the other man's forehead. He dropped to his knees, the gun falling from his hands.

At the top of the stairs, Lisandro turned right while Stephen and Gus went left. Room after room revealed only vacant furniture, but when Lisandro's hand dropped onto the door handle of the final room, it stuck. Rummaging around in his coat pocket, he pulled out his own set of skeleton keys and slipped one into the lock.

Click.

The door opened, and he stepped into a dimly lit room. On a bed in the far corner lay a body, still, as if dead. His heart stopped for an instant. Was he too late? Had they killed her before answering the door?

When the body moaned and turned over, it was all he could do not to sink to his knees in prayer.

"Oh, *gracias padre celestial*," he whispered, and made the sign of the cross.

He hurried over to Maria, halting for a second when he caught sight of her face.

You are as beautiful as a I remember. Thank god you are still alive.

He bent and gently shook her by the shoulder.

"Maria de Elizondo Garza wake up. Maria, we are here to take you home," he said.

His pleas were in vain. She was either in a deep sleep or had been drugged. Lisandro assumed the latter.

Gus appeared in the room and came to the bedside. "At least one person is still alive in this house. I'm afraid you and Stephen are too handy with a pistol, and none of the kidnappers have survived."

It was a pity. Lisandro would have loved to spend some time with the late Señor Alba and find out who had been the mastermind behind abducting Maria. Mister Wicker had probably been the one to collect the first ransom and give the second letter of demand to the priest in Bilbao, but from the indiscreet way the Englishman had behaved in the tavern at Zarautz, Lisandro had concluded he was likely only a middleman. Whoever had come up with the plan to kidnap Maria remained hidden.

Stephen entered the room. "The rest of the house is empty. Toby counted the numbers right." He glanced at Maria and winced. "I assume she has been drugged once more."

Lisandro wrapped his arms around Maria's limp body and hauled her off the bed. Taking her right hand in his left, he draped it over his shoulder. Then, with his head under her armpit, he wrapped his arm around the curve of her knee. Lisandro squatted and Stephen helped to position Maria over the back of his shoulders. Gus stepped in and steadied things as Lisandro stood.

They headed for the stairs and slowly made their way down to the ground floor and out into the rear yard. Within minutes, they had Maria safely on board the coach and were on their way to Gracechurch Street.

Lisandro held her in his arms; between now and when he finally handed Maria back to her family, he intended to keep her with him at all times.

No one said a word. They had rescued Maria, but three men lay dead in the house at number nine Queen Anne Street. Any notion of celebrations was muted in light of those deaths.

They were close to St Paul's Cathedral when Maria finally stirred from her drug-induced slumber and stared up at him. Her eyes were glazed. "Please let me go," she pleaded, her voice slurred.

Lisandro brushed her hair back from her face and whispered softly, *"Estas seguro conmigo."*

She shook her head. "How can I be safe with you when you have stolen me from my family?"

"Maria, it's Lisandro de Aguirre. I have you and I will protect you."

She raised a hand and gave him a feeble punch on the arm. "You kidnapped me. You dirty lowborn *bastardo.*" And with that, her eyes rolled back in her head and she slipped into unconsciousness once more.

Stephen chuckled at him from across the carriage. "Oh dear, there goes any hope you might have had for her thinking you were a hero."

Lisandro took in the sleeping form of the woman he had just rescued.

It was going to be a long and difficult journey home.

Chapter Eleven

Maria woke to real sunshine. There were no curtains blocking out the light—nor was there a foul-mouthed Englishwoman demanding that she rise and shine.

Her head pounded, but she had become accustomed to the daily hangover from the drugs. Her fingers reached out and touched soft, warm blankets. She was sleeping beneath clean sheets.

Is this a dream?

She was surely back home, waking in her bed. Any minute now her maid would come knocking on the door and ask if she wished to take her early morning coffee out on the terrace.

The crackle of wood burning had Maria rolling over onto her side. In a nearby fireplace burned a bright, inviting flame. She focused on the fire surround. It wasn't like any of the stone ones at Castle Vill-abona. This one was wooden.

Where am I?

She slowly sat up her head still woozy.

"Oh," she sighed.

She took in her surroundings. Sometime during the night, she'd been moved yet again. But why? *Has the ransom been paid? Am I going home? Or are they going to kill me?*

The small but functional fire sat to one side of a solitary window. The windowpane itself was plain glass, but from the amount of dirt which clung to the outside of it, she doubted anyone could see in. The whole place had a barely clean feel about it.

She glanced to the other side of the room. A chair. A table. A man slumped asleep on a tatty old leather sofa.

Maria scowled. *Is that the Duke of Tolosa? I think it is. Why is he here?*

Hazy memories of a darkened coach and being carried over his shoulder swam into her mind. Of course! He must have been the one who had masterminded her kidnapping. Her family's sworn enemy had snatched her from the beach in Zarautz and stolen her away to England.

She leapt out of bed, frantically seeking something large and heavy with which to bludgeon him. Maria swore under her breath. There wasn't even a poker by the fire that she could use as a weapon.

A quick check of the door revealed it to be locked.

Of course, it's locked. He might be evil, but he isn't stupid.

She considered the sleeping form of Lisandro de Aguirre. His ruffled dark hair, that stubble which had stirred her secret desires the night of the ball. Why did such a terrible man have to be so damn handsome? In all the folktales, only misshapen and outright ugly ogres were unkind and cruel.

Then her gaze settled on Lisandro's coat pocket and the key ring which was sticking out an inch. Her mouth went dry. Could she do it? Steal the key and make good on her escape? There may well be other men just outside the door, but she had to risk it.

Taking a deep breath to settle her nerves, Maria inched one step toward him. Then another. At the fourth step, a loose floorboard creaked, and she froze. Her gaze remained on him, watching for any sign that he might stir from sleep. He didn't move a muscle. His slow, even breaths continued.

Thank god.

Bending, she hooked the tip of two fingers under the ring of keys and then gently pulled. The keys shifted.

I can do this.

The next tug had them almost free of his coat.

A large male hand grabbed a firm hold of her wrist. "You need to work harder at your pickpocketing skills if you are to make a living as a light-fingered thief," he said.

Maria tried to pull away, but Lisandro held fast. Swinging his legs over the side of the sofa, he sat up. "Now I am going to release you from my hold, and you are going to take a step back. Is that clear?" he said.

She nodded.

Lisandro let go of Maria's wrist. She did take a step back.

And then she launched herself at him. "*Te odio, perro sucio!*"

The first slap landed perfectly on his cheek. She followed it up with a solid punch in the middle of his face which had her hand exploding in pain. "Oh!" she cried.

He rose from the sofa, blood pouring from his nose. He quickly pulled out a handkerchief from his pocket. Maria reached for it, thinking he was about to offer it so she could wrap it around her injured hand; instead, he held it to his face.

"You beat me, call me a dog, and then expect me to be a gentleman?" he said.

There was a rattle and jangle of keys at the door, and it flew open. Two men burst into the room.

"What the devil is going on?" asked the first, his accent marking him clearly as an Englishman.

The second took one look at Lisandro and quickly put a hand over his mouth. Maria frowned at the mirth which danced in his eyes. What sort of man would find any of this amusing?

She backed away as far as she could from them. This morning was the first time she had woken feeling semi-clear in her mind. That clarity of thinking, however, was a double- edged sword. It left room for fear.

Who were these other men, and what role did they play in the Duke of Tolosa's evil scheme?

Tears pricked at Maria's eyes as the weight of her circumstances settled heavily on her shoulders. Her kidnappers had revealed themselves—and with that came the deep worry of why they were no longer concealing their identities.

"Please. My father has money. He will pay whatever ransom you ask," she said.

Lisandro removed the cloth from his face. The bleeding appeared to have subsided.

"Doña Maria, we are not your kidnappers. Last night, we raided the house in Queen Anne Street and rescued you," he said.

Rescued?

She shook her head. It was an unlikely story. How could she believe him?

"Then why is it that you, my family's enemy, is here? Don't tell me you just happened to be in London. Don de Aguirre, I don't believe in coincidences," she replied.

She and Lisandro locked gazes and Maria stared him down, determined to show that she was not afraid.

The look on his face oddly appeared to be more one of concern than anger. His brow knitted tightly.

The tall man who had been first through the door dipped into a low bow, startling her. "I am Sir Stephen Moore, Doña Maria. Lisandro here is telling the truth. We killed three men last night in order to secure your release. No one here is going to hurt you."

Her gaze drifted to the other man. He bowed his head. "I am Lord Harry Steele. My father is the Duke of Redditch. I might be many things, but a kidnapper of defenseless women is not one of them. My wife wouldn't allow it."

He nodded at Lisandro and slyly grinned. "Though from the mess that is my friend's face, I would suggest perhaps that you are not entirely unable to defend yourself."

Maria's fingers curled tightly into balls. She wanted so very much to believe them. That she was no longer in danger and might finally be going home.

Lisandro reached into the pocket of his waistcoat and took out a gold chain.

"My Santiago medallion!" she cried.

But how could he have come by it? I left it at the villa.

Her knees went from under her and she collapsed onto the floor, tears streaming down her face.

Lisandro bent and pressed the necklace into her palm. "Gentlemen, could you please give Doña Maria and I a moment alone?"

He dropped down in front of Maria and wrapped his strong arms around her.

Please, Lord, let this be real. Let this man be all that he says he is.

Chapter Twelve

W hen Lisandro began to softly stroke her hair, Maria lay her head against his chest. The warm comfort of his embrace was too much to resist.

"Here, let me help you." He gestured to the necklace.

She sat back on her heels, and he took it and slipped it over her head. With a sobbed sigh, Maria lay her fingers against the medallion. *I was a fool to take it off. I will never do that again.*

"Did my father give this to you?" she asked.

He brushed away her tears with the pad of his thumb. Shivers thrilled down her spine at his tender regard. "No. Diego did. He doesn't think your father would have ever agreed to let me help with your rescue. I can understand why. With the feud between our families, his honor would not permit it."

The fact that Diego had sought assistance from the Duke of Tolosa still didn't make sense. From the little that she did know of him, Lisandro was nothing more than a well-heeled farmer. And while he had reputedly helped return King Ferdinand to the Spanish throne, he had only been one of many people in that fight.

Why, then, had her brother gone to Lisandro in his hour of need?

After helping Maria to her feet, Lisandro stepped toward the door.

She took hold of the sleeve of his coat. "Don de Aguirre. Forgive me for attacking you. And also, for calling you such dreadful names."

To her surprise, he laid his hand on hers and gave it a gentle pat. When their gazes met, she caught the hint of a smile on his face.

"I should have been on my guard. As I recall, when you realized who I was that night at the ball, you were more than a little disgusted," he replied.

Maria winced, remembering her haughty treatment of him.

His lips spread into a grin. "Come, let's get a spot of food and coffee into you, Doña Maria. I expect you would appreciate eating a hearty breakfast while knowing that it has not been drugged."

He reached for the door handle, but once again, she was reluctant to leave the room. To break this private moment. "Don de Aguirre, you have saved me. And as much as it might disappoint my father, that makes you my friend. Friends call me Maria," she said.

His whole face softened, and tears threatened her once more. "Maria," he said. "And if we are friends, then I am Lisandro."

With an unexpected lump in her throat, Maria followed Lisandro out of the room. They were friends. For now.

But the time may come when they went back to being enemies.

Chapter Thirteen

He was surprised at how much English Maria could speak. Lisandro had been expecting to play translator for her, but not long after she'd taken a seat at the long, well-worn dining table, she was holding her own in a conversation with Augustus Jones.

"I love the coast along the Cantabrian Sea; it so beautiful. And, of course, your delightful village of Villabona. The wines in that part of Spain are magnificent," he said.

Gus placed a hand on Maria's arm, and Harry gave Lisandro a *look*. Augustus Trajan Jones had a silver tongue to rival even Casanova. His list of female admirers was long and illustrious.

Lisandro and Harry were standing side by side next to the fire, warming themselves. It might have been autumn in England, but it was much colder than Spain. Why anyone voluntarily lived in this chilly country was beyond him.

Harry's wife, Alice, had kindly provided Maria with a fashionable warm gown and shawl, along with woolen stockings and a small case containing ribbons and a hairbrush. Lisandro was pleased to know that people who had never even met Maria were still keen to make her feel cared for and comfortable.

The door to the main room opened and Stephen stepped through, followed by young Toby. The boy always seemed to be trailing close behind his guardian. They quickly started clearing plates and cups away.

When the table was free of breakfast dishes, Stephen turned to his young protégé. "Toby, make your introductions," he said.

The boy slipped the cap from his head and came to stand in front of where Maria sat. He bowed low. Lisandro turned away, stifling a laugh as Toby counted to three a little too loudly before standing upright.

"Do . . ." Toby faltered, then glanced at Stephen. A patch of red appeared on each of his cheeks.

"Doña Maria. Remember to curl your tongue like we practiced," said Stephen.

Toby tried again. "Don . . . ia Mari . . . a. I am Toby," he said.

A smiling, Maria held out her hand. "It is an honor to meet you, Toby. I understand you played an important part in my rescue last night."

The boy's eyes went wide, as did his smile. He bounced up and down on the balls of his feet. "I saw you throw the food out the window. And I watched the dog eat it and fall asleep. I was the one who found you."

Maria beckoned him forward. She kissed him softly on the cheek. "You did a wonderful job, Toby. I cannot begin to thank you enough for being so brave. When I get back to Spain, I promise to send you a reward."

He immediately shook his head. "No. Your rescue was enough, Doña Maria."

She glanced over at Lisandro, a questioning expression on her face.

"Sir Stephen is teaching Toby to be a gentleman. And a good man does not always seek payment for his gallant deeds," he explained.

Toby shifted uneasily on his feet once more. His constant fidgeting was evidence that he would rather be anywhere else than there. Stephen placed a friendly hand on his shoulder. "Go and have some breakfast. And when you are finished, make sure you take some nice crispy bacon down to your new dog. Off you go. Good lad."

The boy let out an audible sigh of relief and headed toward the kitchen.

When he was gone, Maria turned to Stephen. "Is he your son?"

"No. When I went to finalize my late father's personal matters a little while ago, I found Toby at the old estate. I brought him back to London with me," replied Stephen.

By-blows and bastards were not the sort of thing one discussed in front of a gently bred noblewoman. There were enough familiar features shared between Toby and Stephen for Lisandro to have come to the conclusion that they were likely half-brothers. From what he had discerned of Maria, she was no fool, and would probably also put two and two together.

Stephen pulled up a chair and took his place at the head of the table. Harry and Lisandro moved away from the fire. While Harry sat on the opposite side of him, Lisandro seated himself next to Maria.

"Now, we know the three in the house are dead. What we don't know is if there is anyone else in London who was directly involved in the kidnapping," Lisandro said.

Maria sat forward. "What about the woman? The one who used to feed me."

Harry cleared his throat. "She received a visit from me late last night, and I took her back to the house in Queen Anne Street. Suffice to say, after having seen her accomplices, she decided to leave town and visit family in the country. I don't expect she will return any time soon."

Maria's cheeks went a horrible gray. Lisandro shot Harry a disapproving look. *Did you really need to tell her that? I am sure death is not the sort of thing she is used to discussing over her morning coffee.*

"Good. She should be grateful you didn't shoot her as well. I would have—given half the chance," replied Maria. She met Lisandro's gaze, and he was the one to blink. Maria de Elizondo was fast changing his opinion of her. Perhaps she hadn't lived such a sheltered life after all. "Lisandro, you are mistaken if you think I have not seen violence. Or that my life has not been without tragedy."

To his ever-growing worry, she then turned her attention to Gus. "Mister Jones, I take it your trips to Spain over the years were not simply to take in the vista. I know the English were heavily involved in my country during the war, and I don't just mean in the battles of the Peninsular conflict. May I be frank with you?"

A clearly uncomfortable Gus gave a nod.

"Did you and your friends act as spies? Agents of the British Crown?"

"Hmm. I don't think I can in all honesty tell you too much of what we did during the war against Napoleon." He glanced toward Lisandro. "And when I say we, I include the Duke of Tolosa in that group."

Maria barely flinched at the revelation, giving Lisandro even more cause for concern. How much did this woman know about his wartime activities?

"Perhaps Maria and I could discuss Spanish domestic politics at another time," he ventured. *Please take the hint. This is dangerous ground you are treading on, Maria.*

She gifted him with a smile. "Of course."

A collective sigh rippled around the gathering. When Gus produced a satchel from under the table and began to pull out various pieces of paper, the knot of tension in Lisandro's neck lessened.

"Since we don't know who else is involved in this kidnapping, I think it is too risky to bring my yacht up the Thames. There may well be people in London, *dangerous* people, who are on the lookout for any sign of Maria being taken out of England. My recommendation is that the boat sails from its usual port of Portsmouth instead," said Gus.

Not for the first time in his life, Lisandro gave a silent prayer of thanks that his smuggler friend owned a private yacht. Smaller boats were handy for slipping in and out of countries, especially when one didn't want to have to deal with the authorities or the pesky issue of import duties.

"Agreed. If we go from Portsmouth around to Bilbao and then overland, I think that will give us the best chance of remaining undetected for as long as possible," replied Lisandro.

Maria slowly turned her head and met his gaze. From the tight set of her jaw and lips, she wasn't as sure as she'd seemed only a minute ago. "Do you really think there are others who would risk trying to kidnap me once more?"

The moment had come to tell Maria a little more of what had happened while she was in the hands of her captors. Lisandro didn't want to frighten her, but she had to know what they would be facing on the long and dangerous road home.

"There were men involved in your capture in Spain, and they remain at large. I met several of them in Zarautz, which is why we won't risk trying to sail into that port. The matter of the ransom is also still yet to be settled," he said.

"So, my father never paid it? I wasn't sure if the masked man was telling the truth when he made mention of the money. In my few moments of clarity, I had wondered if this was payback for something my father had done rather than just a simple kidnapping," she replied.

Stephen leaned forward, hands folded, and frowned. "What do you mean?"

Lisandro held up one hand. "Wait, let's keep to the topic of discussion. Maria, your family did hand over a significant ransom, but instead of you being returned to them, a second demand for money was made. The kidnappers wanted another two hundred and fifty thousand pesos."

"*Increíble! Demente!*" she cried.

He couldn't disagree. It was a huge sum of money. Something beyond the means of most noble families, though perhaps not the Elizondo clan.

"Now you understand why Diego came to see me. His concern, of course, being that even if your family paid the second ransom, there was no guarantee it would secure your release. And that was before any of us knew you had been taken to England," he replied.

Maria shot to her feet. "My family do not know I am here?!"

Lisandro rose and stood next to her. "I sent word to your brother just before I sailed. I trust that he will have told your parents something of your whereabouts."

"But not your involvement or why he chose you," she replied.

"Likely no. When Diego came to Castle Tolosa, it was without your father's knowledge."

"Because of our feud?" Maria said, but her tone was heavy with mistrust.

"Or was there another reason?"

You are clever, Maria. And I appreciate an intelligent woman.

"Your father seems to have concerns about who he could trust at Castle Villabona."

A look of shock appeared on Maria's face, but to her credit she kept silent.

I promise that in time we will find out who the traitors are in your father's house.

This deed will not go unpunished.

Chapter Fourteen

Time was of the essence. Getting Maria back to Spain was the highest priority for everyone.

More than anything, she wanted to go home and see her family. To let them know that she was alive and safe.

Two days after her rescue, Lisandro helped Maria into a small travel coach and then climbed aboard after her. Stephen and Gus were riding shotgun on the roof of the carriage. As a father-to-be, Lord Harry stayed behind in London with Toby. The boy had protested about being left out of the next exciting instalment of the rescue adventure, but Stephen was adamant he would not be exposed to any further danger.

Maria, wrapped in one of Gus's spare woolen coats, the shawl draped over her legs, settled into the corner of the coach. "How long will it take for us to reach Portsmouth?" she asked.

"It's a good eighty miles, so a day or so at a fair clip. Stephen's estate is on the way and we can overnight there. Rest assured, every-thing that can be arranged to ensure your safety is being done. Anyone who wants to question Stephen or Gus's aim with a rifle is in for a nasty shock," he replied.

He pulled two pistols out of his coat and tucked one in the door pocket on either side of the carriage. Her gaze took in the rifle which was already nestled under the bench on which he sat.

From the way he and the others had been passing knives and small pistols around just before they left the offices of the RR Coaching Company, she wouldn't be surprised if Lisandro had at least another three or four weapons hidden on his person. There was comfort in knowing that any enemy who might seek to attack them would be met with unrestrained force.

As the coach pulled out of the yard at the rear of Gracechurch Street, Maria sat forward and gave a farewell wave to Toby and Harry. She would forever be in the debt of these people—strangers who had risked their lives to save her, people she now considered friends.

"I am still going to send Toby a gift once I get home. Not as payment, but as a token of my appreciation. Sir Stephen wants him to be a gentleman, so I think a Cuenca carpet would be the perfect thing for him," she said.

Lisandro raised an eyebrow. "That's a princely gift."

She arranged her skirts and gave Toby one last wave goodbye. "Well, considering that he was the one who first spotted me throwing the food out the window, then observed what it did to the dog, I think it only right."

Lisandro chuckled softly.

Maria was pleased that the boy and the dog would come out of this little adventure better off—Toby with a fine woolen rug; the bulldog, Snick, a new home.

"I must admit to thinking the name he gave the dog is a little strange. What exactly does the word 'snick' mean?" she said.

"It's an old Dutch word. It means 'to cut.' The bulldog is meant to be a combat dog, so I think Toby went with something along those lines. Though with hardly any teeth and one missing leg, I would suggest Snick's fighting days are well over," replied Lisandro.

It seemed the dog was settling quickly into the RR Coaching Company family and was already in grave danger of becoming chubby. Every time Maria saw the animal, someone was slipping it a tasty treat.

"Speaking of payments, are you going to tell me what Diego is paying you for this rescue mission? I don't expect you are doing it out of the goodness of your heart," she said. She had learned to trust Lisandro to a certain extent, but considering the history between their two families, Maria was sure he would be extracting some form of reward for his efforts. Why else would he risk his life by coming all the way to England to rescue her?

He scowled at her.

Did I just offend him? No. That is not possible.

Everyone knew the Duke of Tolosa, and his forebears never did anything unless it somehow served their own interests. They might not ever fulfil a contract, but her honorable family certainly did.

"Actually, I told Diego I didn't want any sort of financial reward for bringing you home; I simply wished to be granted permission for you and me to spend some time together. To possibly become friends. I feel that there was a connection between us that night on the terrace, and I would like, with your permission, to be able to further that relationship," he replied.

And Diego said yes?

She turned to gaze out the window, staring hard at the passing streets of London. Lisandro wishing to know her better was impossible. Notwithstanding the ongoing feud, she was also meant to be getting betrothed to the Count of Bera. What could possibly have prompted Diego to agree to such a thing?

Desperation, or perhaps something else? What am I not seeing?

That first night at the ball in Zarautz, Lisandro had affected her. Sitting this close to him stirred those powerful memories once more. Despite how she wished otherwise, her blood heated whenever he was near.

But he is the enemy of my family.

She kept repeating that mantra over and over in her mind, but it no longer stuck as fast as it had always done. Viewing the man, she had been raised to hate as an honorable human being rather than a rogue was difficult. It made her question too many things. It was all manner of uncomfortable.

"Setting aside your strange notions of you and I somehow becoming friends, I still don't understand why you offered to help. I would have thought allowing my family to suffer would be exactly what you would have wanted." Maria gripped the fabric inside the pockets of her coat, twisting it in her fingers.

Lisandro remained silent. The air hung heavy and thick between them.

Please say something.

"I don't think the idea of us being friendly toward one another is strange at all, Maria. I think it quite sound. Let me ask you this: do you know how the feud between our families began?" he asked.

She huffed. Of course, she knew. The dirty, thieving eighth Duke of Tolosa had stolen from her family. Everyone in their part of Spain knew the story. "One hundred years ago, your family committed a great crime against mine. We have been sworn enemies ever since," she replied.

That was as plain as she could say it without making it too personal. Lisandro's ancestors had started it—not him. But the bloodline was still tainted.

To her surprise, Lisandro nodded. "Yes, my forebears did wrong. But from the sounds of it, I think you have been told a different version of the story to the one I know. So, let you and I make a deal, Maria. If we make it back to Spain in one piece, I will tell you the whole tale of the feud. And when you have heard it, you can ask your father if what I have said is true."

She didn't like the way he spoke about the row between the two families. He seemed to take it far too lightly.

If you had any idea as to how many times, we have toasted the destruction of the dukes of Tolosa, you wouldn't think it so amusing.

"Maria, I simply want to return you home to your family. Only a man made of stone could have refused Diego when he came to Castle Tolosa, asking for my help. My reward, if freely given, would be your friendship. As to whether your father wishes to allow you and I to spend time together, I don't think he is in a position to refuse. His honor and that of your brother are dependent on it."

She turned to gaze out the window watching the view as it changed from crowded and dirty streets to open fields. Maria found herself fighting with a new and unexpected reality. She was fast discovering that not only was Lisandro brave, but he was a man in possession of a good heart.

Seeing her enemy as even more than a fair-weather friend went against all that she had been taught to believe. But if, as he suggested, there was another side to the feud, she owed it to herself to find out what it was.

It wouldn't be the first time that a story had gotten legs and become a twisted version of itself as it grew into legend.

Perhaps she and Lisandro could find a way to become friends.

She glanced back at him once more. The interest he had stirred within her at their first meeting, flared up again and she didn't attempt to resist. She didn't want to fight it.

Perhaps they could become more.

Chapter Fifteen

꧁ꕥ꧂

At the end of a long day on the road, after a number of changes of horses, the coach pulled into the entrance of a country estate. The manor was set well back from the London to Portsmouth road. It would be difficult for anyone to try and hide if they sought to approach the house unseen.

As Maria stepped down from the carriage, she stretched her back and shoulders. Every muscle was tight. "Hopefully I will sleep tonight," she said.

Lisandro met her gaze. "Didn't you sleep well last night?"

Maria shook her head. The drugs had done their job while she had been held captive, but it would take time for her body to readjust to sleeping without them.

"Not very well. I am exhausted. I don't expect I will get a solid night's rest until I am safely back home in Spain."

She could also privately admit to still not fully trusting her rescuers. The medallion from Diego had gone a long way to settling her fears, but until she could actually ask her brother what had been discussed between him and Lisandro, she would remain on her guard.

He talks of friendship, yet I feel that there is more to what he and Diego agreed.

Being constantly on edge frayed her nerves. She yearned to enjoy a long, restful sleep under the shade of one of the giant oak trees at her family's home in Villabona. To wake and find her maid bringing her a refreshing glass of sangria.

I just want to be back in Spain.

Stephen and Gus climbed down from the top of the coach. While Gus led the horses around to the rear stables, Stephen headed toward the front door.

He rummaged around in his coat pocket for a key, then turned to the others. "I'm afraid this won't be a warm meal and cheery fireside evening. I only employ a man to come up from the local village once a week to check on the place. Other than that, the house is usually empty."

Maria's heart sank. She had been looking forward to some hot food. But they would have to make do. This was just a one-night stop on the road to Portsmouth. On the road home.

"If you get yourselves inside and perhaps start a fire, I will ride into Witley and see what food and supplies I can rustle up for us. Hopefully, my estate keeper's wife will have done some baking today," said Stephen.

"Good idea," replied Lisandro.

Stephen disappeared around the side of the small manor house, leaving Maria and Lisandro alone at the front door.

They exchanged a shy smile. Maria drew comfort from it. Considering that he stirred strange emotions within her, it was nice to know that Lisandro also felt somewhat awkward when they were alone. She was supposed to mistrust and dislike this man; instead, she found herself secretly longing to be with him.

I wonder if he also senses this odd tension between us. This magnetic pull.

When he held out his hand to her, Maria hesitated. They had spent the better part of the day sitting in silence in the coach. Lisandro had slept for most of that time while she had watched the green English countryside as it passed by.

He let out an obvious huff of frustration. "Since you and I are going to be spending a lot of time together over the next couple of weeks, may I suggest that you consider lowering your guard."

Maria winced as heat raced to her cheeks. "I am sorry. I must appear to be so ungrateful for all that you have done for me. I just don't . . ."

She fought sudden tears as she stared at Lisandro's offered hand. Her sensible self was forever at pains to remind her that she was supposed to mistrust him.

As she slipped her hand into his, Maria consoled herself with the thought that if Lisandro did indeed return her safely home, anything between them would come to naught. That whatever feelings he stirred within her wouldn't matter. Their lives were set on different paths. She was supposed to become the wife of Juan Delgado Grandes.

But changes in circumstances might see your life alter in ways you didn't expect.

She did her best to ignore her heart as it softly whispered.

Take a chance.

At times, dealing with Maria was like trying to handle a skittish horse. Just when he thought she was beginning to relax in his company, she would suddenly pull away. She still didn't trust him, and that bothered Lisandro more than it should.

Anyone would think I was a monster.

He led her into the house. The downstairs rooms were either empty or had a few items of furniture covered by heavy Holland cloths. It was clear that no one lived in the house.

"Let's see what we can find upstairs," said Lisandro.

They wandered around on the first floor for a short time in the fading evening light, searching for candles and tapers. In a small sitting room, they came upon a hearth which had wood and kindling already set to be lit.

"*Gracias a dios*," a relieved Lisandro sighed.

He located a tinderbox, and soon the warmth of a fire had taken the chilly edge off the room.

Gus popped his head around the door a short while later. "Excellent. Just what we need. I've stayed here a couple of times on my way to and from the coast, and always leave a fire ready for when I arrive late at night. There are also some beds made up in the rooms farther along the corridor."

The idea of a comfy bed was full of promise—but Lisandro could not indulge. He had to keep watch tonight.

Thank heavens I managed to get a few hours of sleep in the coach this afternoon.

Gus settled into a chair close to the fire and gave Maria a cheery grin. "Hopefully this is your last night in England, Doña Maria. If we leave early enough in the morning, we should make it to Portsmouth in time for you to sail on the late evening tide."

"Thank you. I am looking forward to going home," she replied.

A short while later, Stephen joined them. He was followed by a middle-aged gentleman carrying a large basket. Lisandro's stomach growled at the heady aroma of hot pie which filled the room.

And a jug of cider and some fresh bread. And cheese. Magnífico.

"This is Mister Granville. He looks after the house for me," said Stephen.

Gus welcomed the visitor with open arms. "And you brought me your wife's famous beef pies! Granville, you are a godsend."

After setting the provisions out on a nearby low table, Granville handed Gus a small glass jar filled with a pale liquid. "Be honest," he said.

All eyes were on the exchange. Stephen chuckled softly. "Here we go."

Gus opened the jar, held his nose to it and took a deep breath. "Hmm. Good structure. Not too acidic. I note a hint of something new. Have you added a cherry or two in?"

Granville grinned. "Plums."

The master smuggler lifted the glass to his lips and took a sip. "Oh. That's good. You are getting better at this."

He offered the jar to Stephen, who held up his hands in refusal. "Absolutely not. The last time I tried any of Granville's homemade brandy I spent a half day lolling about on the floor."

Granville's derisive snort had them all laughing. Lisandro could understand Stephen's stance; a man had to be careful when it came to moonshine liquor. It could be deadly.

Maria rose from her chair by the fire and Granville took a quick step back. He clearly hadn't registered her presence until now. A low, respectful bow was offered.

To Lisandro's surprise, Maria not only returned the greeting, but she held out her hand and took the jar from Gus. "*Muchas gracias.*"

More than one pair of eyes went wide as she lifted the glass to her lips and downed a hearty mouthful of brandy. She swallowed, then nodded. "This is good. The plums could do with a little more crushing, but I think you have the makings of an excellent drink."

She downed some more of the brandy before holding it out toward Lisandro.

Por favor, no.

When he hesitated, she stepped closer. A playful grin sat on her lips. "Come now, Don de Aguirre. You're not going to disgrace our country by not accepting English hospitality, are you?"

He took the jar and, raising it to his mouth, took the merest of sips that he could without causing offence. When Maria lifted a disapproving eyebrow, he was tempted to go back for a second drink. However, duty and his need for sobriety stopped him.

Granville took the jar and emptied the last of its contents down his throat. After a short conversation with Stephen out in the hallway, he left the house.

"Come, let's eat," announced Stephen. "Granville will bring us some fresh bread and cheese at first light so we shall have food for the journey on to Portsmouth." He tipped his head in Maria's direction. "My only regret about this whole adventure is that you and I didn't get to spend more time together, Doña Maria. I have a feeling you would make for some amusing evenings."

Lisandro gritted his teeth. Stephen was far too easy with his smile and affable nature than a man had a right to be when it came to a woman like Maria de Elizondo. The woman *he* had been tasked with saving.

He liked his friends being comfortable with Maria; it made for an easier existence. What he didn't particularly care for was them seeing her as anything other than the woman they had helped rescue. A woman who was his alone to deliver safely home from England to Spain.

Maria could like Stephen and the others, but from a distance. He met his friend's gaze. The look he sent Stephen was clear and primal in its message.

Don't even think about it. I intend to make her mine.

Chapter Sixteen

✦✦✦

The hot supper was exactly what Maria needed. Her belly was happily full and sleep beckoned. She yawned as softly as she could, but Lisandro caught her eye. He rose from his chair.

"Gentleman, I think it is time to . . . how do you English put it? Call it a night," he said.

Stephen and Gus both nodded in tired agreement. Tomorrow would be another early start and then a late sail. The hours in between would be spent on constant lookout for danger on the road.

"Gus, you can take your usual room. Lisandro, would you care to show Maria to the master bedroom?" asked Stephen.

"I couldn't possibly impose on you, Sir Stephen," said Maria. After all that had been done for her, the last thing she wished to do was put their host out of his own bed. As long as no one drugged her, she didn't mind where she slept.

"I won't be sleeping in the house. Someone needs to stay with the horses. We think we left London undetected, but you can never be sure. A lonely house in the country might appeal to some as being the perfect place to stage an attack," said Stephen. He reached into his coat pocket and withdrew a double-barreled flintlock. Lisandro and

Gus both did the same before putting their weapons back into their holsters.

Stephen nodded at Lisandro. "There is a sword under the bed in the master room, and two other loaded pistols in the top drawer of the tallboy. Smuggling is a dangerous business, and more than one of our competitors wouldn't hesitate to relieve us of our valuable imported goods when they are being moved from Portsmouth to London. We don't take chances."

The sight of pistols being checked dimmed Maria's contented mood. For just a brief time, Maria had imagined herself out of danger. She silently chastised herself.

Only a foolish niña would think she was safe, even with these men.

Embarrassed, she lowered her gaze to the floor. No doubt the sooner the English were rid of their burdensome guest, the happier they would be.

That will leave you in the hands of Lisandro. Alone with him. At sea. For days.

"Come, Maria. Let's get you to bed," said Lisandro. She knew he said it as a matter-of-fact instruction but hearing him say her name and bed in the same sentence had Maria biting her bottom lip.

"I will wake you all when Granville arrives with our breakfast," said Stephen.

Maria and Lisandro bid the rest of the group a goodnight and headed out into the hallway. Candle in hand, Lisandro led her to the end of the landing and through an ornately carved door. She stepped into the master bedroom and he closed the door behind them, locking it.

Maria's gaze went from the key to Lisandro. *Why is he locking himself in with me?*

"I know this is well outside the boundaries of acceptable arrangements between two unmarried people, especially in our country, but it has to be done. You take the bed and I will rest on the couch," he said.

He pointed toward a long sofa on which a blanket and pillow had been placed. She nodded. There was no point in arguing. If Sir Stephen Moore was going to spend the night sleeping in the stables in order to ensure her protection, she had no right to complain about a comfortable bed or the pistol-wielding man sharing her room.

She also liked being this close to Lisandro. The way her heart beat just a little faster whenever he was near had become a pleasant and very welcome sensation.

He crossed to the window and peered outside. After a quick check of the locks, Lisandro closed the curtains. For someone who was supposed to be just a farmer, he appeared quite familiar with measures of security.

Maria yearned to know more about this intriguing man. "Lisandro. What did you do during the last days of the war against the French? Did you fight at Waterloo alongside the English? I know some Spaniards did," she said.

He scratched his forehead and sighed. "I am not at liberty to tell you those things. Not because I don't trust you. But, the political situation in Spain has changed somewhat since the war and with the return of King Ferdinand to the throne. If I told you what I was doing during those years it might put us both in danger."

His words set her on edge. "You mean further danger. I thought our lives were already at risk."

Lisandro headed over to the tallboy and opened the top drawer. He took out two pistols and laid one on the top of the dresser. The other was still in his hand when he returned to Maria's side.

"Yes, further danger." He went quiet for a moment, leaving Maria to stare into his deep brown eyes. He slowly blinked. "How is this for an agreement? When we are on the boat, you and I should discuss the true situation in our country. One thing I can tell you is that your father is no more just a farmer than I am. Both of us are political creatures."

"But you are much more than that, Lisandro. I find myself wanting to be with you and discovering who you truly are," she replied.

A look of desire flitted across his face. "And believe me when I say I would love to learn all there is to know about you, Maria. But first, we have to make it out of England."

He reached out and brushed his hand over her cheek. A chill ran down Maria's spine at his tender touch.

This is wrong. I shouldn't feel anything for this man.

The longer his fingers lingered on her rapidly heating skin the more muddled her mind became. Her sense of self was rapidly diminishing by the second.

It took a great deal of effort, but Maria finally summoned the strength to draw back.

Papá.

Maria had always known him to be involved in local matters of importance; it was part of his role as Duke of Villabona. The idea of him being any sort of player on a larger stage took her by surprise. It also had her worried. What if his activities were the reason for her kidnapping?

"What do you mean when you say my father is a political creature?" she asked.

A guarded look appeared on his face. "Your father played a part in the return of the king to Spain, as did I. But Diego tells me your father has now fallen from royal grace. Perhaps Antonio has regrets about helping the king. He wouldn't be alone in that thinking if he did."

A man who found himself questioning his loyalty to the king could find himself with very powerful enemies. People who would seek to do him and his family harm.

"You think the king may have had a hand in my kidnapping?" she asked.

"We can't put it out of the reach of possibility. Others may seek to win His Majesty's favor by striking at possible enemies. King Ferdinand has plenty of supporters in England. And with you being stolen away here, it means that if anything bad did happen to you, the blame could not be easily laid at his feet."

"Oh. You mean I would never be found."

Lisandro wandered over to the sofa and unfolded the blanket. After checking the pistol once more, he set it down on the floor. He then produced the other pistol from out of his coat and placed it next to it. Both weapons were within easy reach. He took off his coat, but left the rest of his clothes, including his boots, on.

Ready for any possible attack.

"Try and get some sleep. We have a long day ahead of us tomorrow," he said, resting his head on the pillow.

Maria lay on the bed for a long time, mulling over Lisandro's words about a possible motive for her kidnapping. While she wished it was impossible, the longer she thought about it, the more it made bone-chilling sense.

She rose up on one elbow and their gazes met. This man had risked a great deal to rescue her.

"Thank you, Lisandro. If it wasn't for you, I wouldn't be here tonight. I may even be dead."

Lisandro waited until Maria fell asleep and was softly snoring before leaving the room and heading out onto the balcony. He closed the door quietly behind him. The only light, apart from a crescent moon, was the golden glow from Gus's cigar. As Lisandro stepped into the night air, he was greeted with the click of a pistol, then a sigh.

"Better not shoot you," muttered Gus as he un-cocked his gun.

"My future children thank you," replied Lisandro. He came and stood beside his friend, their backs to the wall while their gazes searched the darkness. "Do you think we were followed from London?"

Gus shook his head. "I made certain to check behind us every few miles. If I were a kidnapper intent on overtaking us, I would have done it closer to the city where I could call on more men. To be honest, I think the real danger now lies ahead of you."

In Spain. Where Maria and I will be on our own until I can get her to Castle Tolosa.

He would just have to hope that they could slip into the port of Bilbao and not be noticed.

"Maria settled in for the night?" asked Gus.

It was an innocuous enough question, but Lisandro well knew the real meaning behind it. Maria had been light-hearted when Mister Granville was here, tasting the brandy and showing self-confidence.

But years of war and subterfuge had taught them both that people often adopted a mask when nervous or seriously worried.

"She was asking about her father. Wishes to know what he has been involved in," he replied. *And whether his political affiliations have had something to do with her kidnapping.* "I told her we can talk about it once we board the yacht to Spain. I figure if she hears the truth of what her beloved padre has been doing, Maria might need a few days at sea to be able to absorb that hard truth."

Gus handed Lisandro the cigar, and he took a long, deep drag before handing it back. "I can imagine it might be difficult to accept that Antonio de Elizondo is in fact one of those who have been moving behind the scenes in an effort to curtail the king's power," replied Gus.

"A woman of such noble birth as Maria should only be having to concern herself with finding a good husband and raising a family. She most certainly shouldn't have to worry about being kidnapped. If someone takes issue with her father, that is who they should be dealing with," said Lisandro.

He was not looking forward to having a full and frank conversation with Maria about what was happening behind the scenes in Spain, or how capricious their king could be when it came to matters of loyalty and treason.

Maria's kidnapping might only be the beginning of her family's troubles. It was yet another good reason for the two families to finally set their long feud aside. If he and Antonio could find a way to work together, they might be able to protect both the Elizondo and the Aguirre clans from powerful and as yet unknown enemies.

Only then could Lisandro look to win Maria's heart.

Chapter Seventeen

T he night and the following day passed without incident. It was a welcome respite. As the coach drew near to the coast, Lisandro dropped the window down and let the refreshing sea breeze fill the carriage.

He grinned at Maria across the narrow space. For the first time since her kidnapping, real hope sparked in Maria's heart.

If they could make it safely onboard Gus's private yacht, there was a good chance of her getting back to her family in one piece.

"What day is it?" she asked.

"Sunday. And in answer to your next question, no we don't have time for church. But if you like we could spend a moment or two in prayer together," he replied.

Maria removed her Santiago medallion necklace and held it, while Lisandro placed his hands over hers.

"Por favor, padre celestial, te ruego que mantengas tu buena gracia sobre los dos,", she said. They both made the sign of the cross as Lisandro added. "Amén."

If she made it home safely, she planned to spend time giving thanks in the Elizondo family chapel.

They reached Portsmouth in the early evening and made straight for the dockside. She had been expecting them to stay in the harbor until the tide was ready, but Lisandro and his friends had other ideas.

As soon as the coach came to a halt next to the stone pier, Gus and Stephen both climbed down, weapons at the ready. Lisandro grabbed his travel bag, which also contained Maria's few possessions, and opened the door.

"Wait here for a moment; we need to check that the area is safe. I trust you know how to handle a rifle?" he asked.

Maria lifted an eyebrow in reply. She was a Spanish noblewoman from the Basque country; of course, she knew how to use a rifle. Bending, she lifted the weapon Lisandro had stored under the seat and examined it.

"If I need to fire it to save one of our lives, you can rely on me," she replied.

Lisandro nodded. "Maria de Elizondo, the fortunate man who gets to be your husband will always know that he can count on your bravery."

She sat back on the bench seat and stared at the rifle. It would be wonderful to be married to someone who saw her value. A man who looked beyond her bride price and family name.

Perhaps a man like Lisandro de Aguirre.

He brushed a hand down her cheek, and she met his steely gaze with a resolved heart. She would do whatever he asked.

"Be ready to fire the rifle if you have to. I will be back shortly," he said, and stepped away from the coach.

It was only a minute or two that he was gone, but to Maria, the seconds ticked slowly by. When the handle of the coach rattled, she raised the rifle, ready to shoot.

Lisandro appeared in the doorway and, after giving an appreciative nod, took the weapon from her hands and disarmed it. "The coast is clear. Let's go."

The dockside was empty of other people. Apart from a small rowboat, there were no vessels to be seen. Maria searched the harbor, frowning when Gus pointed to a yacht moored some way offshore.

"The sooner you are onboard my ship, the better, but we will have to row out to it," he said.

Maria's gaze fell on the rowboat and her stomach lurched. She had never been one for the sea, and the idea of getting into such a tiny craft made her want to be ill.

With a tight smile firmly painted on her lips, she turned to Stephen. He wouldn't be making the short trip out to the yacht; rather, he would remain dockside, rifle at the ready.

"Thank you for all that you have done for me. I don't expect you and I shall ever see one another again, but please know that you and Toby will always have a place in my prayers," she said.

He held out his arms and gave her a brief but hearty hug. "I am just glad that you are on your way home. And that you have Lisandro to protect you. As for not seeing us again, you are sadly mistaken, Doña Maria. Before we left, Toby had already informed me of his grand plans to come to Spain next summer."

I owe so much to that little boy.

Eyes brimming with tears, she turned and accepted Lisandro's hand as he helped her down into the boat. Gus cast the line off and climbed aboard. Maria sat in the bow, grimly holding onto the sides with both hands. Stephen lifted his arm and waved farewell; the best she could manage was a nod.

Before they had moved away from the small dock, he turned and headed back to the coach. As the boat slipped from shore, her last sight of him was Stephen rifle in hand looking toward the stone roadway which led down to the water.

"Ready, and pull," cried Gus.

He and Lisandro were seated side by side, each with an oar in their hands. Maria took in long, slow breaths, then let them out again as the boat sailed out of the protected dock. The occasional loud huff from either Lisandro or Gus soon became the only noise which rose above the slapping of the waves.

When they finally drew alongside the yacht, Gus scrambled out of his seat and tossed a line up to one of the sailors onboard. A rope ladder was thrown down to them.

Maria accepted Lisandro's hand and he pulled her to her feet. With arms wrapped around her waist, he then lifted Maria up to the ladder. "Put your foot on the first rung and your hands either side, gripping the rope. Then pull. I will be behind you, making sure you don't fall," he said.

She might well have been a gently bred noblewoman, but Maria de Elizondo was experienced in the art of riding. Climbing the ladder was very similar to putting her boot into a stirrup and getting onto a horse. In fact, she found it was easier. She would challenge any man to get into a sidesaddle as elegantly as she quickly managed to get onboard the yacht.

With her feet firmly on the deck, Maria breathed a sigh of relief. While the yacht itself wasn't an overly large vessel, it appeared sturdy. The crew, who were bustling about, all seemed to know their places and tasks.

This should make it all the way to Spain. I hope.

Quick introductions were made to the captain. She was just beginning to feel comfortable when Gus and Lisandro shook hands. They then embraced in a back-slapping hug.

"Next time don't take so long to come to England. And make sure you arrive ready to stay for more than a few days. Monsale and George will be most disappointed that they have missed you this visit," said Gus.

The thought of it only being her and Lisandro facing the long road home had Maria's nerves back on edge. *I hope that these days at sea will allow us to talk and build on our budding friendship.*

Gus turned and bowed low. "Doña Maria, thank you for being such an excellent hostage. It was a pleasure to rescue you. I hope we shall meet again someday, preferably under less dramatic circumstances." He righted himself, then leaned in and whispered in her ear, "Take the time while you are at sea to consider your future. You could do a lot worse than Lisandro. And don't think for one minute that he isn't watching you with more than just your safety in mind. I think you may have stolen his heart."

Maria's gaze shifted from the chopping waves to the overcast sky, and then back to Gus. She looked everywhere but at Lisandro. "Thank you. And yes, I will take your advice and give that matter much consideration."

She moved away from the side of the boat as Gus gave Lisandro one final hearty slap on the back. "Take care and make sure you return this young woman safely home. We shall see you again, Don de Aguirre."

The master smuggler climbed down and back into the rowboat. For an average-sized man, Augustus Jones was in possession of a strong set of shoulders. Within minutes of taking his leave, he was well on his way back to shore.

Lisandro glanced at her. "There goes someone used to hastily fleeing in a rowboat late at night. He is built strongly as an ox. Come, let me show you down to the cabin."

Down?

Maria quickly surveyed the deck once more. Unlike a proper ship, the yacht didn't appear to have a captain's cabin on the weather deck. In fact, apart from the mast, ropes, and sails, there was little to be seen topside.

Lisandro met her gaze. "No point in having a nice fancy cabin up top if the local militia or navy are firing at you. Much safer to be below deck."

Below deck. Small spaces. Oh dear.

She swallowed deep, forcing the first signs of panic down as best she could. With more than a little reluctance, she followed Lisandro as he headed for a nearby ladder. Every rung that she stepped on was a descent into fear, and a battle against a rising tide of nausea—one she thought she may lose.

When they reached the main deck, Lisandro pointed toward a small cabin.

"That's yours. I hope you will be comfortable enough in it," he said.

I have wardrobes bigger than that.

Her cabin, if one could call it that, was barely a door and a thin bulkhead comprised of alternating slats. While it would afford Maria some privacy, it would also hem her in.

It's like a tiny prison cell.

Reaching out, she took hold of Lisandro's coat sleeve. "I have to tell you—I am not good with small spaces. They give me nightmares, and I tend to wake up screaming," she said.

"Good to know. Thank you for telling me. I will be sleeping in a hammock just outside your cabin, so if you have any problems during the night you only have to open your door and I will come to your aid," he replied.

Maria studied his face for a moment. What was it with this man? Every time she posed any sort of issue, he always seemed to be able to find a solution. Nothing she asked for ever appeared to be a problem. *Remind me again how it is that you are the enemy of my family?*

"Let's go back up on the weather deck. We will be setting sail shortly; you might want to give England your final goodbyes," he said.

As soon as her head cleared the main deck and she was able to breathe the fresh sea air again, the tension in her neck and jaw eased. Grinding her teeth was a nervous habit she had never been able to overcome.

While the crew busied themselves about the yacht, she and Lisandro stood gazing back at Portsmouth Harbor. In the distance, she fancied she could see Stephen and Gus waiting on the shore, still protecting her.

"You have the finest of friends. I don't think many people would be able to count on such loyalty or bravery from even their own family," she said.

"Yes, they truly are good comrades. But don't think for one minute that they are not capable of misdeeds. Every one of them is up to his neck in some sort of dirty business," he replied.

She glanced in his direction. "Something tells me that they might say the very same thing about you. You are loyal and brave, but it takes a particular kind of man to be able to do what you did at the house in Queen Anne Street. To risk your life for someone else. I don't expect that was something you had planned for your life when you were a boy."

Lisandro's gaze remained fixed on the shore. "Sometimes you have to make decisions which lead you in a different direction to that which you had planned. The war with Napoleon did that for many of us, including my English friends. What is happening in Spain at the moment will make other men have to face similar choices."

And women. Don't forget that Spain is our country too.

They moved to the bow of the ship, out of the way of the sailors who readied the ropes and canvases. The sea breeze was stronger here and it whipped Maria's hair about her face. She attempted to tuck her wayward strands behind her ears, but it was to no avail—the wind was too strong.

Lisandro shifted to the other side of her, sheltering Maria from the gusty turbulence. They were close enough now that her shoulder brushed against his coat sleeve. Lisandro slipped his arm free and wrapped it around her. Maria leaned in against him.

Neither spoke. This moment didn't call for words. It was as if a curtain had been pulled back, giving them both a glimpse of what a future together could look like. And as they silently stepped through that doorway, she knew this was what she wanted. They would never again be strangers.

Gus's words came back to her mind. *"I think you may have stolen his heart."*

She had stopped fighting the knowledge that Lisandro was the man who could give her a different life to the one she had so recently thought was her only destiny. In Lisandro's arms she would always be safe.

But as much as she now trusted him to protect her, Maria was no wilting flower. Whatever lay ahead, she was prepared to fight alongside him. Without the others to protect them, she was determined to be someone he could rely upon. For him to know that she would fire a pistol without hesitation, if it came to it.

"Gus said that we would face more danger when we got back to Spain." She broke free of his embrace and turned to face him. "I need to know what you think might happen. Please don't keep me in the dark. Give me a weapon if you need me to wield one."

He nodded. "We are sailing into Bilbao; it is the only major port where this yacht can berth without raising too many suspicions. I couldn't risk Zarautz even though it is closer to Castle Tolosa."

"Castle Tolosa?"

"I am not taking you home to Villabona. Diego and I agreed that until we know who is behind your kidnapping, it would be safer for you to remain hidden at my home."

She stared at him, mouth agape with shock. No one had made

mention of this before. "What did Diego tell you? He must have his suspicions."

Lisandro glanced over his shoulder back down the deck. The crew were well out of earshot.

The expression on Lisandro's face was grave. He closed his eyes, then let out a slow breath. "When you and Señor Perez were attacked on the beach. Did you see him fall?"

Maria flinched at the unexpected question. She had made mention to Lisandro and his friends about the morning she was taken, but they had never fully discussed it. Other than having a sack thrown over her head and then being knocked out, she hadn't thought there was much else to add.

While she searched her vague memories of that morning, Maria's gaze drifted to the wooden deck of the ship. She focused on a nearby coil of rope, tracing the lines as they wound round and round.

"I saw him knocked down. He didn't get back up. I thought at the time he might be dead, but Diego told you he was still alive, that he had recovered." Lifting her head, she met Lisandro's gaze. His face was still set hard. "You cannot be thinking what I think you are. That's impossible."

"Your brother believes his innocence too, but none of us can be certain what really did happen to him. The fact that Señor Perez was found wandering the beach in a daze later that morning has always raised questions in my mind," he replied.

She shook her head in disbelief. How could a man she had known most of her life be involved in the plot to kidnap her? Her father trusted him. Had given him a position of great honor and responsibility within the dukedom.

"But they attacked him. I saw it," she said.

The plea in her own voice had Maria putting a hand to her lips; she didn't want to think the worst of Señor Perez. But why had he been so insistent on them taking a walk along the beach? And it had been his idea to go over to the boat and ask about clams.

Tears pricked her eyes as she drew in a shuddering breath. This didn't make sense.

"Can I suggest that you saw what you were meant to see? I expect the blow was real but possibly not as hard as you might have thought. My experience of kidnappers is that they don't usually stay their hand when it comes to innocent bystanders," he said.

"I am not doubting you, but if this is possibly true then why didn't you or Diego speak to my father? As far as I am aware, Señor Perez is still in a position of great power within Castle Villabona."

The moment the words left her lips, realization dropped into her mind like a stone into a pond. Of course, no one had made a move to accuse Señor Perez of any wrongdoing. If he was indeed involved in her kidnapping, the last thing her family would want to do would be to put her in greater danger by having him arrested.

"Until we can get to the truth of the matter, we need to leave Señor Perez where he is. The man may be innocent. But if he is in league with the people who stole you, we must keep your rescue a secret for as long as we can," replied Lisandro.

"And if he is innocent, we don't want to go accusing a favored family advisor. Someone who has served not only my father, but his country," she said.

The mere notion of having been betrayed by a man she considered a de facto uncle struck deep in her heart. She could only pray that Lisandro had the wrong of it, that someone else was behind it all.

But the seeds of suspicion and doubt had been sown.

A sense of great weariness settled over Maria, her only comfort coming when Lisandro reached out and drew her into his arms. With her head resting against his chest, she stared out over the dark blue waters of Portsmouth Harbor, barely noticing when the ship began to move. Being this close to Lisandro was as natural as breathing.

She had long thought about making it home to Castle Villabona. To what she had always thought was her one true place of safety. Now, with the worry over Señor Perez and other unseen foes, it no longer seemed such a refuge. She and Lisandro were moving from danger and possibly toward greater peril.

There are enemies in my father's house.

As the English coastline slowly disappeared into the distance behind them, Maria turned to Lisandro. "Promise me something, will you? Tell me what is happening and when we are in real danger. If death is coming for me, I would like to know before it arrives."

He took her hands in his and met her gaze. Steely resolve shone within his eyes.

"There are many miles between here and your home. Anything could happen to us on the road ahead. But I promise I will let you know the moment we are both about to die, because, Maria de Elizondo Garza, I will still be fighting to protect you as I take my very last breath."

Chapter Eighteen

hree days later
Off the coast of France

The yacht, which was poetically named *Night Wind,* was well provisioned. After Maria and Lisandro had enjoyed a supper of French cheese and bread, the captain brought them a bottle of burgundy and two tankards.

"The weather is fine tonight, so we could take these up on deck and enjoy watching the sun as it sets," said Lisandro.

Maria smiled. "Yes, that would be lovely."

She found herself smiling at him far too easily. Within the first day of their departure from England, they had settled into a comfortable, familiar routine.

During the day, if the sun was shining, they would sit up on the weather deck, talking to various members of the crew and, when he was not busy, the ship's captain. Maria still privately grinned at the memory of the man's face blushing bright red when she made mention of the yacht's usual purpose for sailing to the continent. Anyone would think the captain had been completely oblivious to the fact that Gus used his private vessel for smuggling contraband into England.

Maria stopped as she reached the top of the ladder and took in a deep breath. The sea air was salty and invigorating.

Being below was warmer, but it still made her uncomfortable. She doubted she would ever get used to the low roof and closed in space. Her tiny cabin was the worst.

On the deck, Lisandro had a quick word with one of the yacht's crew and they both grinned. He gave the man a friendly pat on the back. The sailor tipped his hat to Maria before moving away to carry on with his work.

Lisandro was so easy with people of all rank. The cheerful way he dealt with the crew added to her already well-formed opinion that Lisandro de Aguirre was indeed a noble man. When the exact moment had occurred in which she stopped thinking of him as being a villain and came to view him as an honorable, decent person, Maria couldn't recall. Every day she found herself liking him more and more.

The gentle affection she felt for him was growing, blossoming into something else. She treasured these moments, not wanting to think about the time when this would all come to an end.

A slightly sheepish Lisandro ushered her toward the rear of the yacht to the private spot which they had claimed over the past few days. It was behind several large crates and was one of the rare places on the deck where they could shelter out of the wind.

His skillful fingers soon had the cork out the bottle, and with Maria taking up her assigned role of cup holder, Lisandro poured them both a generous amount of wine. Resting the bottle between his legs, he raised his drink to her. Maria followed suit.

"*A tu salud*," they said in unison.

The first gulp of wine hit the back of her throat and she coughed. Lisandro reached out and rubbed his hand over her back.

We are so comfortable with one another. Like peas in a pod.

She didn't want to consider what lay ahead for them in Spain, but she knew the time would soon come when they would be forced to face the reality of their respective lives. Of the fact that Lisandro would eventually have to return her to her family.

He frowned at her. "Why the long face?"

She pointed her cup toward the land, which sat far off the portside. "France will eventually become Spain. This journey will soon be over. I am wondering what the coming days will bring."

He brushed his hand on her cheek. "Do not be afraid, Doña Maria. I have sworn to protect you and that is what I will do."

"Will you tell me of your plans? I mean for how we are to make it safely from Bilbao to Tolosa. It is a long way by road," she replied.

He took a sip of his wine and stared out to sea for a moment. Maria valued the fact that Lisandro often took the time to consider a response to a difficult question. He could be impetuous in the right moment but never flippant.

"If we make it into port any later than first thing, I plan for us to stay overnight in an inn. I need to go and speak with the head priest at Santiago Cathedral. He may be able to shed some light on the people behind your kidnapping. Then, the following morning, I will hire a coach for us, and we can leave. It is not ideal, but I want to talk to the priest," he replied.

"Do you think people will be waiting for us in port? I mean, news of my escape will reach Spain eventually, but we must have some time on our side," she replied.

"Assuming there were other people involved in London, of which all our RR Coaching Company friends seemed certain, then we are probably at best a day or two ahead of anyone who might have in mind to sail after us to Spain. Where those people might make land is anyone's guess. We will need to keep you hidden as best as possible."

She had asked him to be honest with her about the risks and dangers. Now, she wasn't so sure she really wanted to know.

I just wish I could close my eyes and when I opened them again, I would be back in Villabona and this would all have been a long nightmare. But that would mean never getting to know Lisandro. I couldn't ever wish to lose those memories.

Taking Maria's hand in his, Lisandro shifted and turned to face her. "What is this really about, Maria? You know you can trust me."

I don't want our time together to end.

Maria shrugged, unwilling to give voice to her private thoughts. She put her cup of wine to her lips and took a long, deep drink. Hopefully the alcohol would soon have its usual effect and dull her senses. "I'm sorry. I am just unsettled at this time of night. Sleeping below is always a test of my nerves."

Lisandro studied her for the longest time before finally turning away. The expression on his face told Maria everything she needed to know about what he really thought of her last comment. He didn't believe her in the slightest.

She paused, summoning up her courage. "No, that is not all. I just find myself valuing these moments when we are together."

When their gazes met once more, there was a sparkle in Lisandro's eyes. The soft, playful smile on his lips had her heart skipping a beat. "I like spending time with you, Maria. I like it very much."

"But you barely know me," she replied.

He nodded. "Then tell me more about yourself. For instance, what was happening in your life just before you were kidnapped? Diego mentioned the Count of Bera."

Maria sighed; she had done her best not to think about the arranged marriage her father had been trying to negotiate with the Count. It was an odd thing for Lisandro to bring up, but it sparked hope in her heart. Lisandro had been thinking about her and who she was going to marry.

"When we were in Zarautz, my father and Don Delgado Grandes were in discussion about a possible betrothal between him and me. That's where they were when I went for my ill-fated walk on the beach."

"And are you looking forward to this union? I mean, Don Delgado is someone with influence in Spain. He is a close confidante of King Ferdinand. I expect that in the years to come he will become a powerful man," he replied.

I don't want to marry for power. I want to marry for love.

"I am not particularly interested in marrying Don Delgado. To my mind, he is a lesser man than my father . . . and yourself. You are both concerned with your estates and your people, while he seems only motivated by money and influence," she said.

The longer the negotiations over the betrothal dragged on, the happier she was. The Count of Bera's stipulations for Maria's dowry were outrageous—almost tantamount to what the kidnappers had asked for in their demands for her release.

Her father might wish his daughter to marry well, but he would most certainly not bankrupt himself in the process.

Especially now that he has already paid a goodly sum of money to see me released, only to have it fail.

"So, what will happen when you return home to Castle Villabona? Do you think the marriage will go ahead?" he asked.

If she had not been stolen away from her family and country, then perhaps in time Maria might have reconciled herself to a life of being the Countess of Bera. But the past six or so weeks had changed the way she viewed many things and what she wanted for her future.

If there was a chance that she and Lisandro might be together; if she could win his heart, she would take it.

"Considering that the betrothal negotiations have been going on for months with no sign of agreement in sight, I think the chances of me ever marrying Don Delgado are now slim," she replied.

"And if your father continues to remain out of favor with the king, I expect you will soon become less of an attractive prospect in the Count's mind," he said.

Maria narrowed her eyes at him. No woman liked to be told she wasn't attractive, no matter the context under which it was noted. Lisandro had the good grace, or sense, to flinch.

"I don't mean you are unattractive, Maria—far from it. You are a stunningly beautiful woman. Why else would I have tried to make your acquaintance at the wedding celebrations?"

She let him stew in his discomfort for just a moment before offering a forgiving nod.

"Could Don Delgado possibly have been behind the kidnapping? He was dragging the betrothal negotiations out." If he was seeking to curry favor with the king, punishing the Duke of Villabona might be a good way.

"No. Don Delgado is not that sort of man. He would think such a thing beneath him. I do, however, think that hurting your family was the reason for your abduction. If you disappear, then it serves as a potent warning to others who may seek to take a stand against King Ferdinand," he replied.

Lisandro had promised to speak about her father once they were on the boat. Maria was keen to know what information he had in his possession. "Why has the king shut the door on my father?"

A long and uncomfortable silence followed.

"Maria, we are still not safe; and I won't tell you all that I know just in case you fall into the hands of men who might seek to interrogate you. What I can say is that your father has been working with others to restore the constitution that Ferdinand rejected and took away when he came back to power. The king doesn't wish to publicly denounce him for fear of stoking the fires of resistance."

"Which is why he seeks to strike at his enemies through surreptitious means, such as having their daughters abducted," she replied.

Unmasking the people who had stolen her was the only way to show the king that he couldn't strike out at his subjects with impunity and not run the risk of it coming back to hurt him.

"Men such as the Count of Bera will seek to step into the void created by your father's removal from the royal court."

Perhaps that's the real reason why Juan Delgado Grandes was dragging his heels at settling on the terms of our betrothal.

"I expect when I get home all discussions about me becoming the Countess of Bera will be off the table. Not only am I now the daughter of a man in royal disgrace, but Juan Delgado won't want to marry me after I have spent so many weeks away from home in the company of other men," she said.

Their gazes met. In the fading light, his dark brown eyes took on the appearance of two pools of inky blackness. Yet behind them she could still see the warmth of this man. And his honesty. He smiled at her and murmured, "I cannot begin to tell you how much it pleases me that you won't be marrying Don Delgado."

Chapter Nineteen

After they had finished the bottle of wine, the two of them sat on the weather deck and gazed at the stars. "There is the Estrella Polar. See? It never moves from being due north," said Lisandro.

Maria didn't reply. She had been quiet for the best part of an hour, and it worried him. She was a woman not normally taciturn in nature.

"Maria, we will make it. Try not to worry about Spain or what will happen once we make land," he said.

She gave him a tight smile, then pushed back on the cargo crate and got to her feet. Her small nod was accompanied by an, "I expect you are right."

He rose, picking up both the empty bottle and their cups. "Come on. I think you need a good night's sleep. In the morning, things will look better."

They headed down to the main deck.

At the door to her tiny cabin, Maria stopped. Her gaze dropped to the floor and she toyed nervously with her Santiago pendant. Lisandro itched to take hold of her hand. *Please look at me.*

"*Buenas noches,* Lisandro. I hope you sleep well," she said, not meeting his gaze.

Maria turned and went into her cabin, leaving a frustrated Lisandro staring at the door long after it had closed.

He had been hoping to move their friendship forward this evening, to see if the seed of affection which had begun to grow in his heart was possibly shared by Maria. Instead, the night's conversation had revolved around her father, her possible impending marriage, and the secret identity of those who had kidnapped her.

Of course, she is worried about her family. Don't be selfish in thinking only of yourself.

Maria was also clearly concerned with what might lie ahead on the road from Bilbao to Tolosa.

Her mostly silent mood this past hour added to his growing doubt about his ability to win her heart. He had come to view Maria as more than just the woman he had helped rescue. She affected him on a deeper level than mere friendship. He wanted to take her to his home at Castle Tolosa—to make love to her, and for her to never want to leave.

Listen to your own advice and try and get some sleep. See what the morning brings.

After retrieving his blanket from the hammock, Lisandro sat and removed his boots. He hung them from a hook on a nearby upright post before swinging his legs over the side of the bed and lying down. The canvas sides gently wrapped around him, creating a makeshift cocoon. He was safe from tumbling out, but that was where his love affair with the hammock began and ended.

All that swinging did not make for a comfortable sleep. His head didn't particularly enjoy the constant rocking and rolling motion of the boat, and the hammock did little to settle him.

He would much rather be back in his giant ancestral bed in Castle Tolosa. A bed which was ten feet across by nine feet deep. It was smaller than the famous Bed of Ware in England, but it was still magnificent. The only thing it currently lacked was a permanent female occupant, something he wished badly to address.

I want her sleeping safely in my arms every night.

During the nights on the sea thus far, Maria had displayed a habit for wandering out from her tiny space and pacing the floor for a time before going back to bed. She never spoke to him during those nocturnal journeys—she simply hummed softly to herself, muttered a few things under her breath and then retired to her cabin, not to be seen again until morning.

I wonder if she will sleepwalk again tonight.

Lisandro was on the verge of drifting off when the screaming began.

"Nooooooo! Let go of me. Let go. Please!"

He attempted to sit in a hurry, which only resulted in the hammock flipping and tossing him onto the floor. Lisandro landed with a heavy thud. "Oof."

"No. No. I want to go home. Get off me!"

Lisandro scrambled to his feet. He yanked the cabin door open and dashed inside.

Maria was sitting upright, her arms wrapped tightly around her body, her head bowed. All the while she was pleading with an invisible enemy to let her go.

He raced over to the bed, and taking Maria by the shoulders, he tried to rouse her. "Maria. Wake up! Maria."

She whimpered. Her eyes opened as she lifted her head and stared at him, her gaze unfocused.

"Maria, *mi corazon*, it's me. Lisandro," he said.

Her hand gripped the side of his sleeve and she pulled him toward her. "I knew you would come, *mi amor*," she whispered.

He searched her eyes; a pang of disappointment speared his heart when it was clear she was not fully awake.

Of course, she is still asleep. She is dreaming of her imaginary lover. Not me.

For a second time, he gently shook Maria, trying to rouse her from her stupor.

"Maria, wake up." To his surprise, her grasp on his jacket tightened.

"I am awake," she replied.

"Where are you?" he asked. It seemed the only sensible thing to ask, the one way he could be certain that she wasn't simply answering him in her sleep.

"I am on the *Night Wind*, sailing with you to Spain. I had a nightmare and you woke me with your words," she replied.

Taken aback, Lisandro sat on the edge of the bed. If Maria had been awake since he had spoken, then she would have heard him call her sweetheart. It also meant that she had been conscious when she used the words *my love* in answer to him.

She lowered her head for a moment, but not quick enough to hide the blush which stained her cheeks.

Lisandro was torn. He wanted her. The need to make her his had been slowly building over the past week. *No. That's not the truth. Be honest with yourself.*

The burning desire for her had flickered to life the first time he had set eyes on Maria at the wedding ball in Zarautz. And while the knowledge of who she was had forced him to take a step back, she had still been the woman who had haunted his dreams from that night on.

He was also very much aware that she was a vulnerable young woman, far from home and in his care. To take advantage of her under the current circumstances went against all that he had been raised to accept as being honorable.

And yet, even as he pulled back, she would not release him from her hold.

~

The nightmare of being trapped in a tight space had gripped Maria with its icy fingers yet again. Since she was a child, she had suffered from these sleep terrors.

Their roots went deep, firm in the memories of an accident that she couldn't bring herself to ever forget. The only saving grace of them being that at the end, someone had always come to rescue her. Until now, that person had been Señor Perez, the man who had actually hauled her out of the bottom of the well on the Elizondo family estate.

His place in her dream had now been taken by another—Lisandro. He had risked so much to free her from the kidnappers that of course it made sense that he should be the one to feature in her mind's eye as her life's hero.

But even as she tore her gaze away from him, her cheeks burning, Maria knew her emotions were so very different when it came to

Lisandro. She had fallen for him. The words *"mi amor"* had been spoken from her heart.

"Maria. Look at me," he said.

She braced herself for the inevitable kind brush-off. For Lisandro to give her a speech about them being just traveling companions; and anything else that might grow between them would have to wait.

I don't want to hear that I am pushing things too fast. I know my heart.

As she lifted her gaze to meet his, Maria offered Lisandro a gentle, forgiving smile. Whichever way he chose to let her down, she would understand.

"You called me 'my love.' Did you realize that?" he said.

"Yes. And I meant it. Though it's alright, I—"

Lisandro's mouth slammed down on hers, silencing her. He swept her up into a deep kiss which spoke of longing and need. His lips worked over hers in their heated embrace.

Oh, heaven. I never thought a kiss could be like this.

Maria gripped the front of Lisandro's jacket and pulled him closer, determined that he was not going to be holding the reins completely by himself. His tongue touched hers, then retreated. When he came seeking once more, she met him halfway and their tongues began a long, luxurious dance. She never wanted this to end.

A sudden lurch of the ship had them drawing apart. Panting heavily, they sat staring into one another's eyes. Maria was certain that the expression of surprised delight on Lisandro's face was matched by her own.

"Tell me if I have gone too far," he said.

"Not far enough," she replied.

Their lips met once more, and time simply drifted away. Maria held nothing back and her heart rejoiced as Lisandro wrapped her up in his arms and deepened the kiss.

I want this, I want you.

Whatever the future held for them; she would hold onto the memory of tonight.

As the kiss ended, Lisandro whispered, *"Te quiero siempre."*

Maria nodded. If she had her way, his words would become reality. She would be his always.

"Will you hold me until I fall asleep?" she asked.

"Yes."

Under the blankets Lisandro wrapped Maria up in his arms. They snuggled together, and for the first time in many weeks, Maria finally enjoyed a deep and restful sleep.

Chapter Twenty

T he Port of Bilbao, Northern Spain
Ten days after leaving England.

Maria shivered. She wrapped her arms around herself, but she wasn't cold. Her body thrummed with eagerness to be off the boat and on dry land.

From the moment the *Night Wind* had sailed past Cape Higuer on the border of France and Spain, she had been unable to do anything but stand on deck and stare across the water to the Spanish coast.

Just after dawn, she had caught a glimpse of the conical, towering peak of Mount Serantes. They were nearly home.

It was almost midday, and as the yacht sailed through the Port of Bilbao and into the estuary of the River Nervión, a hint of worry crept into her mind. It was some sixty miles from Bilbao to Tolosa. A lot could happen on the road in between the two cities.

Lisandro came to stand alongside her, the wind whipping through his long hair. He normally tied it back with a leather thong but this morning he had not.

Maria grinned up at him. "You are a fine, handsome specimen of

Spanish nobility." She put a hand to her mouth. She hadn't intended to say those words aloud.

"Thank you," he said. He chuckled knowingly. "Never let it be said that you are not an open book, Maria de Elizondo."

His fingers touched hers and they locked hands. Whatever did happen to them over the next few days and afterwards, they were in this adventure together.

"Where do you plan for us to stay in Bilbao?" she asked.

"I know a place not far from Santiago Cathedral. I want to speak to the head priest as soon as possible about the men he dealt with for your ransom. Once I have done that, we will need to hire a coach and make preparations to leave tomorrow."

The plan was for them to leave Bilbao at first light and make for Eibar, some thirty miles away. It would take a huge effort on their part and a number of changes of horses, but the further away from Bilbao they could make it in one day the better. Talking to the priest was the only way they could get a clue as to who was behind Maria's kidnapping, and if they still posed a threat to her here in Spain.

"As soon as the boat docks, we will head to the inn. It is not the best accommodation that you might ever have had but it's clean and out of the way. We should be safe there," said Lisandro.

"If they can manage a bath for me, I don't mind where I sleep," she replied. Days at sea had left her hair dry with salt and her skin badly in need of a good scrub.

If only it was you giving me a bath and washing my hair. Now that would be perfect.

He leaned over and kissed her tenderly on the forehead. Since the night they had first kissed, these moments of gentle affection had become a part of their ever-growing relationship. Of their deepening bond.

"As long you are sleeping in my arms, that is all that matters," said Lisandro.

They had taken to spending their evenings huddled in their private spot on the weather deck, sharing tender moments. Every kiss or touch of Lisandro's hands sent ripples of pleasure and need through Maria's body.

While the nights spent curled up together in the cramped cabin bed were wonderful, she longed for a time when they could have an open discussion about their future. They had not spoken of a life together, but she sensed this was more due to Lisandro not wishing to tempt fate rather than for lack of wanting it. At the moment. they both seemed content with sealing their tacit agreement with soft kisses and gentle words.

But Maria longed for the time when she and Lisandro could become lovers.

She smiled up at him as he kissed her once more.

"You might want to go down to the main deck and collect your things. I have left a leather hat on your bed, and you should put it on before we arrive. We have to assume that someone might be watching any foreign vessels as they come into port, and taking interest in the passengers as they disembark," he said.

Lisandro's words, while reminding her of the possible perils ahead, gave Maria comfort. He was constantly thinking of how best to manage any threat to their safety. But who was looking out for him?

I should be.

"Lisandro, please promise me that you will not take any unnecessary risks while we are in Bilbao."

"Believe me, I am always careful. And unlike in London, I don't have any friends in this city whom I could call upon if we ran into serious trouble."

Until they made it all the way to Castle Tolosa there was no one whom they could completely trust. Who knew how many people had been paid off by the kidnappers? The fact that they had used the head priest of the Cathedral of Santiago as part of their scheme was a clear indication as to how little regard they had for the rules of society.

Lisandro slipped a hand about Maria's waist and pulled her close. She lifted her face, gratefully accepting his tender kiss on her lips.

"I will not do anything that puts us in danger. The visit to the head priest is only so we may gain some understanding of where any threats to us may come from. Unknown enemies are the worst to fight," he replied.

She kissed him one last time, then drew away. "I will go and collect our things."

As she headed toward the ladder which led down to the main deck, Maria stopped and looked back at him. Had Lisandro caught the meaning behind her words? She had said *our* things deliberately, with good reason. Once they were back on dry land, it would be just the two of them.

Lisandro, you and I are in this together. Not just now, but forever.

·

Chapter Twenty-One

The inn Lisandro had chosen for them was in Barrenkale, one of the seven streets of the old town of Bilbao which ran perpendicular to the river. At the end of each street was the original high stone wall which circled the town. At night, the gates of the wall were closed, and those seeking to move in and out of Las Siete Calles had go via the guards at the main gates.

After they passed through the gate, they stepped into a narrow street with tall buildings which towered over them on both sides. Wet washing hung from many high balconies, drying in the warm sun.

"*Soy un tonto*," muttered Lisandro.

Why does he think himself a fool?

"What is wrong?" she asked.

He turned and pointed toward the high wall. "This has always been a safe place when I have stayed in Bilbao. The walls keep everyone in. I have just realized that it also means we have only one way out of here if we come under attack."

Until that moment, Maria had been enjoying the view on the walk up from the river. Now, the ancient walls of the old town no longer seemed so inviting.

They continued up the cobbled street of Barrenkale for a short distance before entering a walkway through a small gate. At the end, they stepped into the yard of the inn. A sign hung over a nearby door with the picture of a blackbird.

"El Mirlo?" she asked.

"Yes, this is one of the oldest inns in all of Bilbao. It dates back to the thirteenth century. It's been around for longer than the wall. Come. Let's see if we can get a room," he replied.

Maria pulled her hat down farther, hiding more of her face, and followed Lisandro inside.

To her surprise, *The Blackbird* was a well-run establishment, and the owner's wife soon had a metal tub brought to their room. A small procession of housemaids, all carrying pitchers of warm water, followed it. Soon, Maria was staring lovingly at the sight of an inviting bath.

After tipping the maids, Lisandro closed and locked the door to their room. "I suggest you take a quick bath. In the meantime, I will go and see if I can secure an audience with the head priest."

Maria sighed with disappointment. She had been hoping to spend a long hour soaking in the tub and then find a good bottle of Spanish wine. After that, a siesta on the bed was in her plans.

With a wry grin on his face, Lisandro came to her. The warm, delicious kiss he set on her lips brightened her mood a little. Maria pressed herself to him. There was a definite hardening of something against her stomach. Temptation beckoned.

Chuckling softly, he stepped back, hands raised. "If you keep playing that sort of dangerous game, we might never make it out of here."

"Would that be such a bad thing?" she asked.

His face became a study of serious intent. "When I make you mine, and I think we both know that it will eventually happen, it most certainly won't be in an old inn. And especially not when the clock is ticking, and I am about to go and see a priest."

He came closer and whispered in her ear, "Your first time will be special. I want to have hours at my disposal when I make love to you, Maria. Because rest assured that when I do have you naked and beneath me, you will climax more than once."

She swallowed deep, shocked and deeply aroused by his words. In her imagination, she had played out a time when he and she were together but hearing him say it with such certainty . . . it was almost too much.

"Will you stay while I bathe?" she asked.

Lisandro shook his head. "I am a man with more than a modicum of self-restraint but even I am not that strong." He pointed at the door. "Just make sure to lock this after I leave."

After Lisandro left, Maria did as he instructed and turned the key. With her back against the door, she closed her eyes.

He wanted her. She would be his and soon.

She stripped her clothes from her body, then slid naked into the bath. As the soapy suds covered her breasts, Maria took hold of one of her nipples and brushed her thumb over it. Her other hand dipped below the water and up between her legs. As she slipped a finger inside her heat and began to stroke, she lay her head back against the tub and focused her thoughts on him—on Lisandro and the delicious things she couldn't wait for him to do to her.

"There is not a lot I can tell you, but I think you are in grave danger if you remain in Bilbao. The man I dealt with showed no respect for me or the Holy Mother Church. And that sort of man is the kind who doesn't fear for his soul," said the priest.

Lisandro set his glass of brandy on the table. He had hoped that the head of Santiago Cathedral would be able to shed more light on the men who had handed him the ransom notes, but it seemed Lisandro's mission had been in vain. The only thing he'd gained was confirmation that it was the Englishman Wicker, whom Lisandro had seen in Zarautz, who had dealt with the money the Duke of Villabona had paid to secure Maria's release.

"When was the last time you saw this Mister Wicker?" he asked.

"Yesterday. He keeps coming to ask if the second ransom has been paid. That is why I think you need to get out of Bilbao, and quickly.

News of your arrival in Spain may not stay secret for very long. Sailors drinking in taverns like to tell tales."

Lisandro got to his feet; decision made. He and Maria had to leave Bilbao, and today. They would get as far on the road to Tolosa as they could before nightfall.

"Thank you, Father. I appreciate your honesty. I am sorry you have been caught up in all this and the grace of the Holy Catholic Church so badly mistreated," he said.

The priest made the sign of the cross in blessing. "Send word once you have delivered Doña Maria de Elizondo Garza home to her family. I shall pray for both of you. God speed, Don de Aguirre."

Lisandro left the cathedral by way of a side door and turned left into Posta Kalea. It was a longer walk back to *The Blackbird* than leaving by the front, but he had suddenly become averse to the crowd which mingled around the cathedral's entrance. In his mind, every person he passed could well be someone linked to the kidnappers.

He had just turned left again, moving in the direction of the river, when his gaze locked on a familiar body. There on a street corner, casually smoking a cigar, stood the badly scarred Englishman, Mister Wicker.

Lisandro's blood ran to ice.

"*Infierno sangriento*," Lisandro muttered under his breath.

He chastised himself. Here he was, still within sight of the cathedral, and what was he doing? Offering up blasphemy.

I am going to go to hell.

Setting aside all worries about eternal damnation, he pulled the collar of his coat up and kept to his side of the street. It was only when he finally made it into a nearby lane and was well out of sight of his enemy that Lisandro allowed himself to breathe a sigh of relief.

He hurried on quickly to the inn. There was no time to waste.

Please be finished bathing and be ready to leave.

Reaching, *The Blackbird*, he slowed his steps. A man rushing anywhere usually created interest. The last thing he wanted was for someone to make mention of a guest leaving in a hurry.

He knocked on the door, pushing past Maria as soon as she opened it.

"Oh!" she exclaimed.

Her startled response pulled him up sharp. He had been so intent on getting back from the cathedral, a thousand worries in his head, he had just barreled into the room and not given her a second thought. The vision of loveliness which met his gaze now gave him pause.

Maria had bathed and dressed. Her long brown hair had been braided and hung over one shoulder. She was a radiant picture of Northern Spanish beauty.

The only thing which spoiled the view was the look of hurt on her face. The pain in her warm brown eyes.

"Forgive me," he said.

She tilted her head to one side and considered him. "What is wrong? You seem terribly agitated, Lisandro. What happened at the cathedral? Were you able to get any information?"

He let out a long, slow breath, doing his best to regain his composure. Maria was right; he was in a state of flux.

"The priest at Santiago Cathedral wasn't able to give me much. But he did tell me that the man who I saw in Zarautz, the scarred Englishman, is here in Bilbao. He is the one who has been handling the ransom letters and your father's money," he explained.

He reached for his travel bag and began to stuff things into it. After picking up Maria's hat and coat, he handed them to her. "We have to leave now. I just saw that same man standing outside the cathedral."

"The Englishman with the burned face? I am sure he must be the same man who put the sack over my head. He knows what I look like, so yes we have to go," she replied.

She came to his side and placed a hand on his arm. "Take a moment and calm your mind. Then let's you and I come up with a sensible plan."

With reluctance, Lisandro did as she asked and let out a long, slow breath. It quietened his racing mind. Lisandro's hands still shook from the rush of adrenaline coursing through his veins, but he could at last think straight.

I can do this. I can get us out of here.

"If we leave Bilbao now, we might make one of the villages en route to Tolosa by nightfall. We stand a better chance if instead of hiring a coach, we avail ourselves of horses," she said.

He went to open his mouth to ask about her horsemanship skills but a hard glare from Maria stopped him. "My father owns a whole stable of Andalusian grays. I was taught to ride a warhorse from the time I could walk. Please don't insult me by asking how well I can handle a mount."

She was smart, resourceful, and if he hadn't already fallen in love with her, Lisandro would have done so at that very moment.

"It is going to be a long and hard ride. I'm sorry that you didn't get a chance to sleep in a proper bed tonight, but once we make it to Castle Tolosa, I promise you will get plenty of rest," he replied.

He was dying to show Maria his huge bed. To roll her in it, make love to her, and then sleep soundly with Maria wrapped in his arms. But Lisandro was determined that Maria's first time would be wonderful, and that for those long hours of tender caresses, her mind would be solely on the two of them.

Right now, however, the threat of her kidnappers still hung over them.

Once he got her safely home to Castle Tolosa, to the home he intended would be theirs forever, then they would be free to indulge in their desires. To become one.

Chapter Twenty-Two

Lisandro glanced up at the dark clouds and swore. Rain was coming, and soon; he could smell it in the air. The last thing either of them wanted was to be caught out on the road in the middle of a storm. They had left the last village two hours ago, and it was too far for them to travel back and escape the threatening weather.

"It looks like we are going to get a soaking," he said.

When he received no answer to his comment, Lisandro drew back on the reins and turned to look over his shoulder. Instead of Maria being where she had been, travelling just a horse-length to his rear, she was a good fifty yards behind him. She had dismounted from her horse and was staring out over a nearby field.

Lisandro rode back and pulled his horse up next to hers.

"It's going to rain soon; I think we should seek shelter. That looks as good a place as any," she said.

His gaze followed her pointing finger. A low stone barn in the middle of a grassy meadow caught his attention. *A granero! Tonto! How did I miss that?*

Not for the first time did Lisandro send a prayer of gratitude to heaven for having been gifted the company of not only a beautiful woman, but a capable one.

They led their horses through a gap in the rock wall that ran alongside the road and toward the barn. There was no sign of a house anywhere. The barn was more than likely a place for hay to be stored and as a winter shelter for animals.

Inside they found exactly what they needed.

"This is perfect. There is feed for the horses, a trough with fresh rainwater, and best of all, clean hay for us to sleep on," she said.

They tethered the horses at one end of the barn, then removed the saddles. While Maria set about unpacking their gear, Lisandro gave their mounts a well-deserved rub down.

"You are mighty beasts and have got us a long way today. I give you my thanks," he said.

Not surprisingly, the horses didn't bother to respond. They were too busy tucking into the clean hay.

Today had been long and extraordinarily arduous. From arriving into port early in the afternoon, to then discovering that their enemies were lurking in Bilbao, to now having spent many hours in the saddle, Lisandro was bone-weary.

If only we had made it to Eibar. I hate us being out on the road like this; it leaves us exposed.

He would have to settle for accepting what progress they had made. Maria was out of Bilbao, and Eibar was close enough that if they had to make a midnight dash for it, they stood an even chance of success—so long as the threatening storm was not fully upon them.

With the horses dried and fed, he joined her over in the corner of the barn where she was sitting on a pile of loose straw, cutting up some cheese. Earlier in Bilbao, while he had been negotiating the purchase of two horses, Maria had gone to a nearby market and secured provisions. For a daughter of nobility, she was possessed with a sensible and practical nature.

From the saddlebags, she produced a sealed ceramic jug of cider, a large loaf of fresh bread, and a jar of pickled vegetables.

"That looks delicious," he said.

She grinned at him, then produced another small sack and handed it over.

Lisandro opened it and took out a long object wrapped up in cloth. His nose picked up the scent in an instant. "Smoked cod?"

"Now we are truly back in Spain," she said.

Lisandro leaned over and placed a soft kiss on her lips. "That we are."

It may have been simple fare, but with Maria by his side, it was the best meal Lisandro had enjoyed in a long while.

The rain came an hour later, heralded by lightning and thunder. A cacophony of noise danced across the tiled roof of the barn. Fortunately, the horses seemed to be comfortable with the drama from the heavens and paid it no heed.

In their cozy corner of the barn, Lisandro and Maria huddled over a small lamp. It was the only source of light they dared use. They hadn't seen anyone on the road for several hours, but they couldn't risk being discovered. If they had been followed, a secluded barn in the middle of nowhere was the last place they wished to be found.

The very thought of Lisandro making good on his promise to fight to the death in order to protect her had Maria blinking back tears.

I can't bear the thought of ever losing him. I love him.

He passed her the last of their remaining food. Maria wrapped it and placed it back into the bags, along with the rest of their provisions. Lisandro then carried them over to the saddles. Everything was ready just in case they had to make a hasty escape.

When he returned to her, Lisandro sat and took Maria in his arms. Using a pile of clean straw, she covered them to help keep warm. The barn was dry, and they were as comfortable as the circumstances would allow.

"We should try and get some sleep. I know the weather is bleak, but I want us to be on the road at first light," he said.

She looked at him and smiled. "How far is it from here to Tolosa?"

"Somewhere around twenty-eight miles. The horses are both in good health and are capable of doing it. I know it will mean another long day in the saddle, but the sooner I can see the tower of my home, the better. I have men who can take up arms if required," he replied.

Despite Lisandro's suggestion, Maria didn't want to sleep. Not just yet. The mention of his family home provided the perfect opportunity to engage him in conversation.

"Tell me about your home. I mean, what it means to you," she said. She didn't need him to describe the place; she would see it for herself soon enough. What Maria wanted to know was how it had helped to form the sort of man that Lisandro was—someone who looked beyond his estate to the rest of Spain.

Lisandro lifted the glass of the lamp and blew out the candle. They were plunged into darkness. The only source of light were the occasional flashes of far-off lightning as the thunderstorm moved away.

"I expect it is similar to yours in many respects. Crops, beans growing on hillside trellises. I have a small amount of wine grapes growing on the southern side of the estate. I intend to add some more sheep in the next year and go back to making cheese."

A warm kiss touched her forehead and she sighed. "Go on."

"My home is the reason why I got involved with the English during the war against France. I wanted Spain to be free of Napoleon, to be able to make its own decisions regarding the future," he added.

Those were much the same words her father had said during the dark days of King Ferdinand's exile in France. That a free Spain was what all of them wanted.

"But having the king once more on the throne is not going to achieve that. He has gone back on his word. The ordinary Spaniard has been left without hope or rights," she said.

Her words were dangerous—some would say seditious. Traitorous. His silence was just as worrying. Had she just said something which could get her into further trouble?

You know men don't like to hear women discuss politics.

"You should be careful about what you say, Maria. Ferdinand has already had many people arrested this year—writers and newspaper editors. He intends to crush any sort of opposition to his claim to absolute rule," he replied.

"So, you would wish your future wife, whoever she is, to be silent when it comes to these sorts of matters?" she said.

In the inky night, it was impossible to read his face. His hand took hold of hers and soon soft kisses touched the palm of her hand. "No. But I would expect that she used careful judgment when it came to be expressing her opinions and with whom. There are dark days ahead for Spain. King Ferdinand is a capricious and vengeful man. There are courtiers who would seek to win his favor by telling him the names of those whispering words against him."

"You were one of the people who helped bring him back to Spain. My father also," she replied.

The reality of their situation set her mind on edge. Her father, too, had worked to restore the king to power, but now he was out of favor.

Spain was changing, and she feared it was not for the better. What if she had given her heart to a man who fought to maintain the status quo when all the world around them was shifting?

"I did what I did because I am a loyal Spaniard. But since his return, Ferdinand has proven himself unworthy of being king. I would suggest your father has come to the same conclusion. All I ask of you is that if we discuss these sorts of matters that it is done in the privacy of our home, and even then, not in front of the servants," he replied.

She caught the warning in his voice. Who was to say that one of Lisandro's trusted household members wouldn't turn against him in the same way as they suspected Señor Perez had done with her father?

Lisandro would be branded a traitor and publicly denounced. She couldn't bear the thought of him being taken away to Madrid and having to face the royal inquisitors.

"Agreed. We will only talk about this when we are alone," she said.

He was a part of her life, and she would do anything to keep him safe. Maria rolled over and placed a tender kiss on Lisandro's lips, then whispered, "I trust you to do what is right for this country, and I will always stand beside you. I love you."

"I love you too."

Chapter Twenty-Three

❦

The first glimpse of Castle Tolosa's tallest tower had Lisandro reining in his horse. He let out a heavy sigh. He was almost home.

Relief coursed through him. Just a mile or so more and they would have made it. The long weeks since he had set out for Zarautz seemed an eternity ago.

The gentle clip of horse's hooves on the dry, hard road had him turning as Maria pulled her mount up alongside his. She held a hand to her face, shielding her eyes from the dying rays of the setting sun.

"Is that it?"

Suddenly caught up with emotion, Lisandro could only nod in response. He had been on edge for so many days that the tide of utter relief threatened to overwhelm him.

She leaned over and patted him on the knee. "You did it. I am so proud of you—and so very grateful."

He swallowed the large lump in his throat. "We did it. You. Me. And those rogue friends of mine in England. Everyone played their part."

With a touch of his heels, he urged his horse on. One of the first things he would do once he got home would be to instruct the master of his stables to ensure that his and Maria's horses were given a full rubdown and housed in the very best stalls with plenty of hay. A fresh apple or two was also on the list.

As they rode slowly through the gate which led into the Aguirre estate, Lisandro stopped and pointed to the town of Tolosa, which was nestled at the bottom of the nearby valley some six miles away. Castle Tolosa itself was situated at the top of a mountain near to the village of Bidania.

Maria clapped her hands together. "And there is the Oria! Oh, Lisandro, I feared that I may never see it again."

The dark waters of the Oria, which flowed through both Tolosa and Villabona on its way to the Bay of Biscay, cut through the country-side like a winding ribbon. It shone brightly in the final light of the day.

When things were settled and safe, he would take Maria to Tolosa and introduce her to his friends and family. He also had in mind to pay a visit with her to the church of Saint Mary and give prayers of thanks for their safe return. While they were there, he intended to have a quiet word with the priest about arranging a wedding, one which would bind the Aguirre and Elizondo families together forever.

But that was for the future. There were still many obstacles in their way. Apart from the as yet unidentified kidnappers, there was also the not so insignificant issue of the Duke of Villabona. Lisandro could just imagine how his first conversation with Maria's father might go.

Don de Elizondo, I rescued your daughter. Oh, and I fell in love with her, and I am going to make her my wife. What was that about an old feud?

They continued on toward the castle proper and passed under the enormous wrought-iron gate. He grinned as Maria glanced up at the heavy barrier which hung overhead.

"Don't worry. The chains that hold it are strong," he said.

Men and women flooded out from the main castle and surrounding buildings. By the time Lisandro and Maria had finally reached the front door, almost one hundred people were following in their wake. But he only had his sights set on one person—the woman dressed in black standing on the front steps.

His mother.

After throwing a leg over the saddle, Lisandro dropped to the ground. He glanced at Maria, intending to help her down, but she shooed him away.

"Go and see the duchess. Don't you get me into trouble with my future mother-in-law before I have even had the chance to meet her," she said.

He knew better than to question Maria in front of the all too observant servants. They were all standing wide-eyed, staring at her. As he made his way toward his mother, the whispers began.

"Who is she?"

"She looks like the daughter of the Duke of Villabona, but that's impossible."

"Could it be her?"

"Whatever could it mean?"

Lisandro smiled and kept walking.

It means a wedding, and an end to a long-running and pointless feud.

Lisandro's mother fussed over Maria just as her own mother would no doubt do, once she returned home. Within an hour of her arrival at Castle Tolosa, Maria had been bathed, her hair had been washed in goat's milk soap, and she was wearing a new gown.

"It might not be the latest of fashions, but my daughter left it here when she visited from Madrid in the summer. I would like you to have it," said the dowager duchess, standing behind her and offering up a warm smile.

Maria considered herself in the mirror. The pale gold, and cream gown was exquisite. It laced up at the back in a way she had not seen before. If the gown came from Madrid, there was every chance that such styling would not reach this corner of Spain for at least another season.

"I couldn't possibly keep it," she replied.

The duchess placed a gentle hand on Maria's arm. "I insist."

The generosity shown to her by the matriarch of the Aguirre family humbled her. These people weren't the evil enemy, as she had been led to believe. Instead, the similarity between her family and this one was quite striking.

"You spoil me, Doña Elena," she replied.

"You are a guest in my home. It is only right and proper that I take care of you. Especially after all that my son tells me you have been through."

She patted Maria's arm. "I shall leave you for a moment's peace. The evening meal will be served shortly out on the terrace."

After Doña Elena had left the room, Maria spent a few minutes alone giving silent thanks to God that she had been saved. Tonight, she would sleep restfully under the roof of the Duke of Tolosa—the man who had risked his life to come to England and bring her safely back to Spain.

With her clothes and hair now perfect, Maria wandered out onto the terrace. The sun had gone down. What appeared to be a thousand tiny torches were dotted around the three walls which enclosed part of the space. The only side of the terrace not walled in showcased a darkened field. Maria could just make out the rows of grape vines in the subdued light.

Her gaze caught a movement out of the corner of her eye. A tall, dark-haired man approached. She swallowed deep at the sight which held her spellbound.

Lisandro.

She had never seen him dressed in such splendor. Even her vague memories of the ball in Zarautz couldn't compare to the elegance of him tonight. His long hair had been washed and brushed back, held in place with a strip of black velvet.

His pure black evening jacket was perfectly offset with buckskin trousers and a white linen shirt. The gold of his vest serendipitously matched her gown. She stifled a grin, remembering that neither of them believed in coincidences.

I wonder who planned that?

She beamed with joy as Lisandro bowed low. "Doña Maria, you are truly dazzling in that gown."

"You scrub up well yourself. For a moment there I wasn't sure it was you," she replied.

He offered her his arm, and they strolled out to the edge of the stone paving. Maria pointed at the nearby vines. "What sort of grapes do you grow here?"

"Syrah. They are a dark red, quite strong in flavor. It's an unusual grape for this region, but I have a palate which likes a full-bodied wine. Some of our local Malaga and Sherry is not to my taste," he replied.

Maria checked behind her, making certain they were alone. She leaned in and kissed him on the cheek. "I've been wanting to kiss you since we arrived. I forgot how things would be once we were back in society," she said.

He chuckled. "And here was me thinking you were interested in the wine. You are a naughty girl. Come here."

Lisandro pulled her to him and took her mouth in a scorching kiss. His lips moved over hers with comfortable familiarity. She groaned when their tongues met and tangled.

Someone loudly cleared their throat. The kiss came to an abrupt end. An embarrassed Maria turned her face away.

It's no longer just the two of you. You can't be careless in front of others.

"Good evening, Mamá. I am pleased you could join us." Lisandro greeted his mother.

The dowager duchess snorted. "I doubt that very much. Or, should I say, you might have been happier if I had left it a few minutes longer to make my arrival."

Maria didn't know what to do with herself. The temptation to run off into the dark and hide in the vineyard was strong. Stepping away from Lisandro, she put space between them.

This was the first time anyone else had been made aware of the romantic relationship connecting her and Lisandro. And while it was inevitable that they would eventually have to reveal their love, this was most certainly not the way she wished her future mother-in-law to find out.

A look passed from mother to son, and it was clear in its meaning. *Are you sure?*

"I intend to make Maria my duchess," he said.

From the first night she and Lisandro shared a room alone at the RR Coaching Company offices in London, this had always been her fate. As an unwed woman of high, noble birth, there couldn't be any other outcome. It didn't matter if nothing had transpired between them; to save Maria's honor, marriage was the only possible solution.

She'd known this—but hearing those words made it feel real. He would be hers. Nothing could stop their union. Love and destiny had worked hand in hand to bring them to this day.

Doña Elena came to Maria and took hold of her hand. There was the hint of a tentative smile on her face. "My son is a good man, and he will marry you because Spanish society and the church will expect it of him. But I want to know the truth of your heart in this matter. Do you care for Lisandro?" she said.

"Yes. I love him," Maria replied.

There was no hesitation in her response. That night on the road, at Stephen's house, she knew Lisandro held her heart. Every day since, her love for him had grown stronger.

"I am glad, but it doesn't address the problem of Don de Elizondo and what he wants. We all know that if he is against the marriage, his decision will be the one which counts," said Elena.

Maria turned her gaze to Lisandro. "If we decide to marry and my father does not support the union, then we will just have to trust that the church will."

Going against her family and marrying Lisandro would be something of a last resort, but she wanted to be clear about her decision. If the Duke of Tolosa wished for her to be his wife, she was willing, family feud withstanding or not.

Lisandro held out his hand to her, and she shyly came back to him. She could only pray that her father would see the sense in all this and finally put an end to the enmity between their clans.

"Do not fret over the future, Maria. All will be well—I promise. We are both tired after such a long journey. So, tonight, let us eat, drink, and enjoy good company. Tomorrow will see a fresh morning and the path ahead."

"But what of my family? You promised to send word," she replied.

"I sent a message to Castle Villabona not long after we arrived. Diego knows that you are safe and back in Spain, though I did tell him we are somewhere on the road from Bilbao. I dared not risk anyone knowing you are here. We still don't know who can be trusted among your family's servants and friends."

Lying to her family did not sit well with Maria, nor was she happy about being kept in the dark about it. A private conversation with Lisandro was in her plans for the latter part of the evening. She might well be in love with him, but Maria had been raised to have opinions of her own, and she would not stand idly by while Lisandro went ahead and made all the decisions in their lives.

Tonight, would be one for sharing honesty and agreeing to the terms of their future marriage. She had a horrible suspicion Lisandro might not like all that she was going to demand of him.

When Elena left the terrace several hours later, Maria and Lisandro shared a few quiet minutes. The evening had gone well. By the time the dowager duchess bade them both a fond goodnight, Maria was greatly relieved to know that she had the blessing of this woman.

Lisandro picked up his wine glass and emptied the last of it. He sat back in his chair and stared out into the night. *A penny for your thoughts, Don de Aguirre.*

He rose from his chair and came around to where she sat. Maria accepted his offered hand and got to her feet. She melted into his embrace as Lisandro wrapped his arms around her.

"You must be tired, my love," he said.

She lifted her gaze and smiled up at him. "A little, but I am more in the mood for a private conversation with you. If you are willing."

He narrowed his eyes. "And where would you wish to have this discussion? Out here on the terrace or . . ,"

"You did promise to show me your giant bed," she said.

When the lines of worry between his eyes grew deeper, Maria softly chortled. Placing a hand on his waistcoat, she toyed with the buttons. One popped open and she slipped a finger inside. The fine, thin linen of his shirt barely created a layer between the skin of her hand and the hairs on his chest. A second finger joined the first and she rubbed them back and forth. "Take me to your room."

Lisandro didn't protest.

Chapter Twenty-Four

This wasn't how he had envisioned his night ending. Lisandro's plans had included a pleasant evening with Maria and Elena on the terrace, then a solid night's sleep in his own king-sized bed. He yearned to slip beneath the sheets and lay his head on the soft pillow. Sleep had almost become a stranger to him.

The moment Maria had flicked open the first of his buttons, he'd sensed she had other ideas. Ones which did not include him sleeping alone.

But Lisandro was not without his own surprises.

Taking Maria by the hand, he led her up to his private quarters and into his bedroom with its oversized bed.

"Oh! That's huge," she exclaimed.

Hopefully that's not the only time you'll appreciate the size of something this evening.

"Would you like to retire to your room?" he offered.

Her grip on his fingers tightened. She had been all smiles and bravado up until this moment. Now, he sensed her sudden hesitation. Her apprehension.

It had been some years since Lisandro had been a virgin, but he could still remember the feelings of trepidation. Of worrying if he would be up to the task. He could just imagine that for Maria those emotions would be greater.

His first time had been an enjoyable tumble with an experienced older woman. There had been no repercussions for him when it became a whispered secret around the household servants that the future duke had lost his innocence. Even his father had privately congratulated him on becoming a man.

For Maria, the stakes were higher.

If he cared for her, he had to give her a way out. A chance to rethink things and wait. Much as he wanted Maria beneath him, if he had to bide his time until they were wed it wouldn't be too much of a sacrifice.

I am not a beast, unable to command my base desires. Besides, when the time comes that we are together, I want her to feel comfortable. To know she is protected by the vows of marriage.

She let go of his hand and wandered toward the bed. Her fingers brushed over the gold and silver silk coverlet. When she turned back to him, determination sat on her face. "I want this. I want you tonight, Lisandro. Make me yours."

He hesitated, offering her more time. "You said you wanted to talk. Perhaps we should do that now before anything else."

She sighed. "Alright let's talk. I was disappointed that you sent word to Diego without telling me what you were going to say. When we marry, you can't keep secrets from me. I need to be able to have some rights in my life, and one of those must be the right to be heard."

Lisandro was so accustomed to making decisions for himself that he'd simply forgotten to take what Maria wanted into account. He would have to overcome that habit. "Forgive my oversight. Maria, I want you to have a voice in our marriage. You were clearly not raised to be a silent partner or fully submissive to the will of your husband. It will take time for me to change long ingrained forms of behavior. All I ask is that you are patient with me," he replied.

From what he already knew of Maria, patience was not a virtue she held in great supply. Theirs would be a marriage frequently tested by two strong wills. He would be a fool going into this union if he thought it would be anything else.

Still, he wanted a wife who challenged him. A woman not prepared to be either meek or mild. Maria would push him to become the sort of man he could be, should be, and she would stand alongside him through thick and thin. Right where he wanted her.

"Thank you. I know I am not an easy person to live with; you can ask my brother when you next see him. What I am is a woman who loves you, Lisandro. I want to spend the rest of my life with you. To bear your children and see the dukedom of Tolosa continue."

After hearing Maria's declaration, Lisandro knew there was only one thing left for him to do. He crossed to the tall set of drawers which sat against the far wall and, after retrieving a small velvet pouch from a box, came back to her.

He knelt on the hard, wooden floor and took hold of her hand. "Maria Isabella de Elizondo Garza, will you do me the greatest honor and be my wife? My duchess?"

Tears brimmed in her eyes. "Yes. My father will probably never forgive me, but yes."

She bent, placing a soft, tender kiss on his lips. Lisandro reached up and brushed away a stray tear. "I am sure the Duke of Villabona will come around. He loves you; he will not forsake his only daughter."

From out of the pouch, he took a ring. A single, bright emerald sat in the center. It was a priceless jewel brought back to Spain from the royal mines in Columbia. Lisandro slipped the ring onto Maria's finger, then kissed her hand.

"Now all we need is a priest and the blessing of the church," she said.

He had promised to be honest with her, and with their betrothal, it was time for him to live up to that undertaking. He got to his feet. "I am going to travel to Villabona tomorrow and speak to your father. Amongst other things, I will be asking for your hand in marriage."

She frowned at him. "I notice you said 'I,' not 'we.'"

"You and I will travel together as far as the convent of Saint Casilda just outside of Irura. I don't want you to remain here just in case something happens to me. Since the convent is on the road to Villabona, if things do work out and I am able to unmask who is behind your kidnapping and have them arrested, then I can return quickly and bring you back to your family," he said.

His biggest concern at this point was the risk to Maria's safety if he suddenly arrived home with her. Whoever was behind her kidnapping might go quiet, deciding to bide their time and wait for another opportunity to strike at the Elizondo family.

He had to draw the enemy out from their hiding place, make them reveal themselves. And in order to do that, he had to put himself in danger.

"Are you sure this is the only way? I mean, I am not disagreeing with your plan. It's just the thought of something happening to you fills me with dread," she said. The betrothal ring had been on her finger for a matter of a minute and she was already gripping it tight.

"I am not going to do anything foolish. Besides they don't know where you are, so no one is likely to make an attempt to kill me before they get you back."

"I don't think my father would try to harm you, Lisandro. You might have an inkling of his politics, but I know him as a man. The two of you are not that distant in your ways," she replied.

Lisandro was going to have to place his trust in the honor and true character of Antonio Elizondo. His life depended on it.

"Well, after tomorrow many things will be settled. Hopefully the day will see us toasting our betrothal. If it doesn't, I will likely be sitting in chains."

Chapter Twenty-Five

A ll this talk of plotting and schemes had Maria thinking Lisandro would want her to leave. To let him get sleep and be ready for the fateful day ahead.

He slipped a hand around her waist and pulled her to him. Maria gasped as the firmness of his erection pressed against her stomach.

"Last chance. You can leave this room right now and we can wait until we are married to make love."

Maria had been sure of her decision before they had talked; now, she was adamant. Lisandro was not leaving Castle Tolosa without having claimed her as his woman.

She brushed a hand against the bulge in his trousers, then took a hold and gently squeezed. "I hear that this is what I am supposed to do. Is it alright?"

He drew in a deep breath and whispered, "Maria, yes."

A long, warm kiss was her reward for giving him pleasure. She groaned as their lips and tongues worked over one another. For a strong, powerful man, he was surprisingly tender when it came to be kissing her.

His hands worked their way up to the bodice of her gown, then around to the back where the laces were tied. He tugged on one of them and she waited for it to come loose. With a hum of disappointment, he tried again.

"These things are wickedly tied," he said.

"Sorry I didn't think to loosen them."

It was hard to think of much else other than her nerves and rapidly beating heart.

She pulled back and turned around, placing her hands on the edge of the bed. "Does this help?"

There was a moment of unexpected silence. She glanced over her shoulder to see him staring at her ass. When their gazes met, he grinned. "I was just recalling the night we rescued you and I had to carry you out of the house slung over my shoulder. In all the mayhem, I didn't get time to appreciate just how magnificent your *trasero* is, so forgive me if I indulge for a moment."

Maria giggled; his indelicate remark was exactly what she needed. Her nerves were on edge, humor the perfect antidote.

Strong arms came around her, lifting her away from the bed. Lisandro blazed a trail of warm, tender kisses down her neck. She shivered at the heady sensation that thrummed through her body as he touched her skin.

"Don't be afraid. I will keep you safe in all things," he said.

"Even this?"

"Yes, especially this."

From the first day they had been together in London, Lisandro's honest nature had overcome both Maria's hatred and mistrust of him. Within days, she had willingly placed her faith, and indeed her life, in his hands.

Giving herself to him tonight was the ultimate act of trust.

Reaching behind her, she searched for the laces of her gown. Her fingers gripped the shortest tie and she tugged it free. Lisandro quickly stepped into the role of lady's maid and deftly loosened the rest of them.

The cool night air kissed her back as he pulled the gown open and pushed the top of it down. Instinctively she held onto the fabric, keeping her breasts covered as she turned to face him.

"Let it go; I want to see you. All of you," he whispered.

Maria sucked in a shaky breath as Lisandro took hold of her hands and drew them away from the bodice. When he gave a hard tug and the gown pooled at her feet she didn't protest. She was bare; only her shoes remained.

Her nipples hardened. The thought of being naked before Lisandro had her pulse racing. Maria lowered her gaze, too shy to look at him. With his hands placed on her waist, Lisandro knelt.

Cupping a breast lightly in his fingers, he leaned forward and drew one tight bud into his mouth. Pleasure tore straight to her core. When he sucked, she closed her eyes and let out a ragged breath. "Oh, Lisandro," she panted.

Her mind barely had time to register the sensation of his firm lips on her nipple when he slipped a finger into her wet heat and began to stroke. Maria's world swayed on its axis. It was all too much to take.

Please don't stop. I need your touch.

He worked her slowly up to a state of sobbing, aching need. Her fingers dug into his shoulders, gripping tight. The man was a master at knowing every place to touch on a woman's body.

Lisandro released his lips from her breast with a *pop*. Rising up on his knees, he continued to stroke her sex.

"That's it. I want you to come this way, Maria. It will make things easier for when I claim you," he whispered.

She was in no state to argue. All her mind and body could think of was reaching the earth-shattering climax which she sensed was just a stroke or two of his fingers away.

He rolled his thumb over her sensitive nib and she crashed into a blinding orgasm, collapsing against him. To her relief, he didn't stop. Instead, he slowed the pace while continuing to stroke her as she slowly came down.

Maria's mind was still in a post-orgasmic haze when Lisandro lifted her onto the bed and, with almost godlike speed, quickly shed his clothes. As he turned back to her, she got her first glimpse of his fully naked body. Her mouth dropped open at the sight of his engorged manhood.

She had seen the horses in the fields near her house, knew the basics of what happened when a stallion found a mare in heat. But they were animals, and her mother had never allowed her to linger and see what actually happened when the well-hung male horse finally got his way.

Lisandro gave her an encouraging grin. "Don't be afraid. I will make this good for you."

She wasn't so sure, given the size of what was pointing large and long at her.

You are not the first woman to share her body with a man. Just try and relax.

He crawled onto the bed and rose over her. Taking her hand in his, he placed it on his cock and held it there. Maria wrapped her fingers around the shaft.

"Now, move your hand up and down. Stroke me like I did with you. Slowly at first. Listen to my breathing and take your cues as to how fast you should go," he said.

"Alright but let me know if I am not doing it right," she replied.

To her surprise, she quickly established a steady rhythm and soon had Lisandro quietly swearing under his breath. When he groaned and whispered, "Maria," she sensed he was nearing his peak.

He stilled her hand and brushed it away. As he positioned himself at her entrance, she closed her eyes.

The sensation of him entering her body was odd. There was a moment of pressure, then it was gone. He withdrew and then pushed in deeper. By the time Maria realized he was fully seated within her, Lisandro was already increasing the pace of their coupling.

Every time he thrust into her, she wanted him to go deeper. The ripples of pleasure began to build once more, and Maria gripped the sides of his hips, urging him on. All she could think of was the need for him to take her harder.

"Lisandro, oh God, that feels so good," she sobbed.

He slipped a hand between them and ran his thumb around her bud. Faster, he worked her with his fingers and his cock. Her growing desperation for release had her clawing at his ass.

Maria lay her head back on the pillow, screaming as she came in a soul-defining climax. Lisandro pounded into her in one final frenzy before he let out a shout and collapsed on top of her.

"Oh, Maria. I will never get enough of you. I love you."

She held him close. "I love you, and this is forever."

Chapter Twenty-Six

They made love once more during the night, and then again just before the dawn. Lisandro had planned to let Maria be after their first time together, to give her body a chance to recover, but she wouldn't allow it.

The last time he had taken her, she'd been spread before him over the edge of the bed while he'd entered her from behind. He had tried to be gentle, but with Maria begging him to take her hard and fast, a man could only say no once before giving in to his base desires. He loved the sound of Maria's cry as he thrust deep into her and she climaxed.

It was mid-morning before they finally stirred from the bed.

"I shall ring the bell for some fresh, warm water. We need to dress and eat before we set out on the road this morning." Lisandro threw his legs over the side of the bed and stood. He playfully batted away the greedy hands of his fiancée. If Maria got a hold of him again, there was every chance she would demand another round of sex.

This minx might well be the death of me.

Maria propped herself up on her elbows as Lisandro tied his dressing gown at the waist. He risked a peek at her breasts, pleased that she was comfortable being naked in his presence.

He swallowed, fighting temptation. It would be so easy to roll her over and spread her legs once more.

And she would let me do it.

"Can I ask about your scars?" she said.

Her words pulled him from his lustful thoughts. He hadn't counted on the scars being a topic for conversation. He was so used to them, he barely noticed them anymore.

"I got most of them during the war, a couple in the past few years. Not every mission goes according to plan. In fact, few ever do. When you are dealing with dangerous people, especially the kind that carry knives and pistols, injuries tend to happen," he replied.

Maria climbed off the bed and came to his side. He leaned over and gave her an easy, loving kiss. It made his heart flip when she was near, and to know that she was this relaxed with him. With them as a couple.

When her hand settled gently on his chest, Lisandro spotted the betrothal ring.

"I think the ring suits you perfectly," he said.

She raised an eyebrow at his obvious attempt at changing the subject. As far as he was concerned, Maria had already been exposed to enough violence and danger. She didn't need to know all the insane things that had happened to him.

A feminine finger traced a line along the scar which ran from his left shoulder to the middle of his back—the result of a fight with a piece of loose metal on the side of a building, rather than a knife.

"The ring is gorgeous, and I will wear with pride. But I want to know more about you, about your life," she said.

"Alright. Choose a scar and I shall try to remember how I came by it."

She touched a hand to the ugly scar on the top of Lisandro's arm and he gritted his teeth. "Tell me about this one."

"I call that my scar of instruction. It was a painful lesson in why one should never listen to a mad Englishman when he offers up dangerous and reckless schemes. We tried to blow up the powder magazine at Fort de Guesclin in Brittany. I got a hot bullet for my troubles," he replied.

Memories of that night still haunted him. Anyone who said that a flesh wound wasn't agony had never truly suffered one. Even thinking about it made him wince.

When Maria touched another of Lisandro's scars, he took a gentle, but firm hold of her hand.

"You must understand that there are some things I can never share with you. Scars which will have to remain a mystery. It's not a trust issue, mind you, Maria; it's because if you knew the secrets behind them it could put your life in danger. We have to think of the future and our children."

She nodded. "I understand. There are things I know my father and brother keep from both my mother and me. They don't do it with any sort of malice, but again to stop us from holding information that could bring us harm."

He was about to walk into the home of a man he barely knew, and whom he most certainly didn't trust. The Duke of Villabona had his own secrets; and for the first time, Lisandro wondered what exactly they were.

"When we were on the yacht, we talked a little about the political situation here and of your father. What we didn't discuss in much detail was my own story. I need you to understand that while I helped bring King Ferdinand back to Spain and for him to retake the throne, I am now finding it difficult to support his reign. What he is doing to those who seek to speak freely goes against my values as a loyal Spanish patriot," he said. There would never be a time when Maria wasn't her father's daughter, but she had committed herself to him. She had to reconcile any differences that may exist between the two men in her life.

"And you know that my father has fallen from grace. The fact that the Elizondo family did not warrant an invitation to the royal wedding in Madrid should be enough for you to know that the king has turned his back on us," she replied.

"Ferdinand is a man capable of holding a grudge, but he may smile upon your father once more. Who knows?"

Maria met his gaze. "I think things may be irreparably broken between them. Papá spoke out against some of the arrests which happened recently. When he tried to raise the issue of restoring some of the powers of the constitution, King Ferdinand threw both his shoes at my father and told him never to come back to the royal palace."

Lisandro had heard rumors of the shoe-throwing incident but had put it down to an exaggerated tale. Now, he was worried. Throwing shoes was a grave sign of insult.

A chill ran down his spine. Had the plan ever been to accept the ransom money and release her?

Nausea threatened. What if he had not gone to the tavern that night? If he had missed the Englishman and then not found the note? So many things could have gone wrong and Maria may never have been found.

"Lisandro?"

He clenched his hands into tight fists. The notion that he might had missed knowing her or winning her love threatened to overwhelm him with despair. This woman had always been his destiny.

"I love you. No matter what happens today, you must know that you will hold my heart always." Lisandro pulled Maria to him and held her tight.

She put her arms around him and nestled her head against his chest. "I love you too. And because of our love, I know we shall succeed."

They held one another for a time, neither speaking. Lisandro went through the plan in his head, refusing to consider the hundred or so ways it could go wrong. Of what today might cost them.

We will not fail. Today, the good and righteous will win.

Chapter Twenty-Seven

Maria managed to hold her nerve steady for the rest of the morning and the short ride to the convent of Saint Casilda. To say that the abbess was surprised to see the Duke of Tolosa and the daughter of the Duke of Villabona on her doorstep would have been an understatement.

"I will ride on to your home and present myself to your father. If things go well, I shall return here later this afternoon. If there is any problem, I will try to send word," he said.

She wiped away tears, determined not to break down. "Diego will not fail us."

"I hope so. Our lives may depend on it."

The response of her brother to Lisandro's secret missive the previous night would be crucial in this final stage of the rescue. Things were already set in motion, and Maria could only pray that Diego would come to their meeting point well prepared for any trouble.

Lisandro patted the side of his coat. Under it was a loaded pistol; the matching one was strapped to his leg. She had sat on the giant bed in Lisandro's room and observed him dressing. Apart from the pistols, there were three small knives hidden about his clothing. The only obvious weapon was his ceremonial sword which hung from the belt around his waist. If anyone tried to disarm Lisandro, they were going to be in for the fight of their lives.

She wanted to be there, standing alongside him when he met with her father, but she understood the best place for her was somewhere where she could be protected. If things went according to plan, and the villains who had sought to harm her were unmasked, there would come a time when she could seek justice.

Lisandro walked over to his horse, and Maria followed him. They embraced one last time and he gifted her with a tender kiss.

She stared into his brown eyes, praying that it would not be for the last time. "You come back to me, Lisandro de Aguirre. I am not finished with you."

"I promise I will. We have a wedding to plan and a life to live together."

He mounted his horse and turned its head toward the front gate of the convent. With a 'ya,' he dug in his heels and the horse quickly rode away.

Maria prayed she would see him again.

Chapter Twenty-Eight

Lisandro didn't look back as he rode out of the gate of the convent. As he'd turned away, he'd caught a glimpse of tears shining in Maria's eyes and he was determined that if things did go awry, his last memory of her would not be one of sadness.

Today I will claim what is mine, and those who have sought to harm Maria shall pay.

It was a little more than two miles from the village of Irura to Castle Villabona. At a gallop, his horse could travel the winding mountain pass in less than fifteen minutes. But once he reached the main road, Lisandro drew back on the reins and slowed his mount. His gaze searched the snaking track ahead.

Trees dotted the steep hillside to his left, while on the other side of the road, the lush, green grassland fell away until it reached the valley floor. Lisandro knew this mountain path well.

Where are you?

He urged his mount on again. Rounding a bend, he caught sight of a group of men riding toward him. He held his breath.

As they drew near, the hooded man at the head of the group raised his hand. By the time the two parties met one another, they were at a walk.

"The Englishman was spotted in the village this morning, and Perez met with him. He is still playing the innocent, of course, but after your note was received last night, the scales finally fell from my father's eyes, mine too," said Diego.

He and Maria had left Bilbao only just in time.

Thank God I saw him outside the cathedral. He must have had spies watching the city gates.

The fateful storm had probably saved their lives, with Wicker not being able to catch up with them in the furious raining maelstrom.

"Good, so Antonio knows not to trust Perez. Maria is at the convent of Saint Casilda, in Irura. If they come for her, don't hesitate to shoot," he replied.

Diego nodded and continued on, his heavily armed troops following. The chink of metal swords accompanying the sound of hooves on the road. Lisandro let out a slow breath of relief. Maria would be safe.

Now it was up to him to entice a rat out of its hole.

Castle Villabona loomed large in front of him as Lisandro reached the top of the small hill. It wasn't as grand a construction as his own home, which gave him cause for a secret smile.

At the entrance to the castle, he surrendered to the armed guards and was taken into custody. His pistols, sword, and most of his knives were seized. The knife he had strapped to his back remained successfully hidden.

He was escorted at gunpoint into the grand reception room of Castle Villabona. The Duke of Villabona rose from his chair.

Lisandro dipped into a low, respectful bow. "Don de Elizondo."

Coming back to an upright position, his gaze fell on the man standing to the right of Maria's father—a well-dressed gentleman whom he immediately assumed was the duplicitous Señor Perez.

El canalla.

With his head of gray hair, Señor Perez even looked somewhat like a rat. When he narrowed his eyes at Lisandro, he knew he had his attention.

His self-confident poise gave Lisandro a moment of clarity. The arrogant way he held himself suggested that he was someone more than capable of organizing and masterminding something as evil as the abduction of his master's daughter.

Lisandro could just imagine what was going on in that cunning, calculating brain. Perez was likely wondering how he could turn this unexpected encounter to his advantage.

"Why is the enemy of my family standing in my home?" demanded Antonio de Elizondo.

Lisandro met his gaze and coolly replied, "I have your daughter, and I want you to pay me a ransom before I consider whether I should hand her back."

There were gasps of shock and horror from several of the people gathered in the room. Maria's father, however, remained stony-faced.

"This is an outrage!" bellowed Perez.

"Call it what you will. I want one hundred thousand pesos, or I will keep her," replied Lisandro. He wasn't going to ask for the same as the kidnappers had, fearing it would trigger too many questions in Perez's mind.

The Duke of Villabona angrily strode over to where Lisandro stood and glared at him. "And just what will you do to my daughter if I don't pay the ransom?"

Lisandro stifled a grin. Maria had come up with a surprising number of sexual things he could offer to do to her when they'd discussed what he should say at this moment, but he wisely kept them to himself.

"I haven't yet decided. Ruining her sounds like a good start. No one, least of all Count Juan Delgado Grandes, will want to touch her after I have had my way. She'll be tainted. Soiled. Call it whatever you like," he replied. He coolly met Antonio de Elizondo's gaze. "Perhaps I could even put my bastard in her belly."

The duke's face twisted into a look of pure rage. His cheeks turned a deep crimson. He shook his fist at Lisandro. "God will strike you down for this, Don de Aguirre. The gates of hell will welcome you to their fiery pit."

"Pay the ransom or let me leave. My men have instructions to kill Maria if I am not returned by nightfall," he replied.

Señor Perez stepped forward and leaned in to speak to the duke. "Let me have him in the dungeons for an hour, Don de Elizondo. I will get all the information we need to rescue Doña Maria. I swear on my life I will not rest until she is safely home."

Lisandro looked him up and down with undisguised disdain. *Just a little more, you, filthy traitor. Step farther into the trap.*

"Seize him. Take him to the cells and make him talk. Torture him if you must," said the duke.

Guards came and roughly took hold of Lisandro. He was dragged from the room and thrown into the dungeons. The solid, iron door was slammed shut behind him.

With his back against the ragged brick wall of the cell, he stared at the door and waited. "Come on, Señor Perez," he whispered.

The trap was set. Now all that remained was for his prey to take a nibble of one last morsel of tasty cheese and it would slam shut.

Chapter Twenty-Nine

Señor Perez did not fail him. Within minutes the cell door opened, and the family servant appeared. Lisandro was not surprised when the man immediately dismissed the two guards who had accompanied him.

"I shall get all that I need out of Don de Aguirre. By the time I am finished with him he will be begging to offer up anything I ask," he said.

The two men nodded and headed back up the stone stairs, the door slamming shut behind them.

"Who are you?" asked Lisandro.

Señor Perez straightened his back and puffed out his chest. *Here we go—the display of self-importance. The establishing of just who is in charge.*

This wasn't Lisandro's first time in a prison cell—nor was it his first time being interrogated. Sir Stephen Moore had spent many hours during the war teaching Lisandro how to deal with being questioned.

"I am Señor Perez. I have loyally served the Elizondo family for thirty years. That is all you need to know, Don de Aguirre," he replied.

This was the perfect opening for Lisandro. If his suspicions were correct, the lure of money and power over the Elizondo family would be too great for Perez to resist.

"Pity. Because if I can get the ransom out of Don de Elizondo, I will be in a position to buy myself some new friends. Friends who could help support the king. And we all know that King Ferdinand likes to reward loyalty."

Perez opened his eyes wide. A look of uncertainty appeared on his face, which greatly pleased Lisandro. It was clear that whatever he had been expecting to hear from his prisoner, it most certainly was not an offer to betray his employer.

Lisandro waited patiently. He knew how the mind of a calculating, self-serving traitor worked. He had met enough of those sorts of men during the war.

"Are you trying to tell me that the Duke of Villabona is not loyal to the crown?" said Perez finally.

A half-shrug was Lisandro's response. He was treading carefully, drawing the man in. "I think we both know that Don de Elizondo has fallen from His Majesty's favor. King Ferdinand is not one for directly punishing people; he prefers more subtle ways. At the same time, he is quietly elevating others to positions of power and influence. And there is always room for men prepared to do the unpleasant work required by the crown."

I don't think I can be more obvious, so for heaven's sake, take the bait.

Señor Perez paced the floor. When he returned to Lisandro, he was slowly raking his fingers through his salt and pepper beard. "What are you offering?"

In his mind, Lisandro could see the edges of the trap. He was sure if he just stretched out his hand, he would be able to touch them.

"Money enough to buy yourself a villa in Madrid and some nice clothes to wear at the royal court. But more importantly, I can arrange a role for you with people close to His Majesty. You would be a man of power and influence. Help me out of here and I can give it all to you." Lisandro scowled and pointed a lazy finger in Señor Perez's direction. "Or have I read you wrong, and you are content to be merely the servant of a nobleman for the rest of your days?"

A sly grin appeared on Perez's lips. From his coat pocket, he withdrew a knife. He held it in front of Lisandro. "It's a tempting offer, but what I really want is for you to tell me where Maria de Elizondo is being held. I know you wouldn't be so foolish as to leave her at your home. Once I have her and the second ransom, I can leave you to rot here."

Lisandro chuckled. "You are exactly the sort of man the king needs in order to control his enemies—cold and ruthless. Maria is at the convent of Saint Casilda in Irura. You should hurry if you plan to snatch her away. Oh, and if you can get the money out of Antonio de Elizondo, you are welcome to it. Ferdinand will reward me with much more than just money once I bring his enemies down."

Perez hesitated for a moment. "What do mean?"

Lisandro gave him a slow smile as victory beckoned. "You didn't seriously think you were the only one making moves against Don de Elizondo, did you? He won't dare lay a hand on me once I tell him that I report directly to the king. In fact, he will beg to release me."

He casually moved his hand to his back and scratched it. Perez's gaze followed but did not linger. He didn't see Lisandro dropping the handle of his knife into his hand. If his jailer intended to stab him, he was ready.

"How well you come out of this is entirely up to you," replied Lisandro.

"Guards. Open this door!" cried Perez.

Señor Perez moved quickly outside, and the clang of the bolt being thrown back into place soon echoed in the cell.

The first phase of Lisandro's plan was now complete. Diego and his men would now have to play their part.

He placed his hands together and with head bowed, began to pray to the Virgin Mary. "*Ave María llena eres de gracia.*"

Please keep Maria safe.

Chapter Thirty

The first of his prayers were answered a short while later. The door of his prison cell opened and through it stepped the Duke of Villabona.

"Perez rode out from the castle not ten minutes ago. The guards informed me that he turned left and headed toward the village. I am assuming he has gone to see the Englishman."

Lisandro nodded. "I told him where Maria was. I also passed your son on the road here, so he and his men should be ready for them when they reach the convent."

The duke sighed. Deep worry lines etched his face.

It was odd to feel pity for a man he was supposed to hate, but Lisandro did. He could well understand why Maria's father looked aged and broken. His only daughter had been missing for near on two months and last night would have been the first time he had been given any real hope that she was even still alive.

"Am I still your prisoner, Don de Elizondo?" he asked.

"No. From what Diego has told me, you might well be my savior. Come, let us go upstairs and wait. If Perez is true to form, he won't waste a minute sending Wicker after Maria."

~

The clop of horses' hooves on the stone flagging of the convent's central courtyard had Maria racing to the upstairs window. She peered out from behind a curtain. A half dozen men, all mounted on Andalusian grays, were gathering below.

She bit on her lower lip as fear coursed through her veins. From their cloaks and the markings on the saddles, she could tell they were her father's men. Her mind whirled with a thousand worries. What if Diego had not been able to leave the castle early this afternoon without raising the suspicions of Señor Perez? Had these men been sent by the traitor, and was she about to be stolen away again?

"Lisandro," she whispered.

The leader of the group dismounted and was met by the convent's abbess. She turned and pointed toward the window where Maria stood.

As the hood of his cloak fell back, she caught sight of her brother. He waved at her.

Diego.

Maria tightened her grip on the curtains, fearing she might faint. He was here. The plan was working. Lisandro would come back to her.

Within minutes, Diego had raced upstairs and into the room. He threw his arms around her and lifted her high. "Oh, thank you, sweet lord. Oh, Maria, I feared I may never see you again."

He set her down and took her face in his hands. "Everything at home just stopped the day you disappeared. Mamá wanders the castle grounds incessantly while Papá spends his days writing letters to people, begging for any news of you."

"Do they know I am safe? That Lisandro rescued me?" she replied.

"They do, though I have not been able to speak with our mother. She read the note last night and then went directly to the chapel to pray. There have been many rumors as to what happened to you. Some say you drowned in the sea that day in Zarautz."

She screwed her eyes closed, fighting and failing to hold back her tears. All she wanted was to go home. To find her dear mother and calm her worried heart.

But there was one last thing they had to do in order to cut the traitorous cancer out of the house of the Duke of Villabona.

"Did you see Lisandro on the road here? He left but a short time ago," she said.

Diego nodded. "We passed each other on the other side of the village. He knows that Papá is in on the plan."

Downstairs, the horses were taken to the convent stables and hidden from view. The heavily armed men that Diego had brought with him were stationed at various points around the courtyard. If anyone arrived to try and take Maria, they would not be leaving alive.

The abbess and nuns left the convent by way of a rear laneway and headed to the nearby San Miguel church for safety.

Maria turned to her brother. "Are you really going to spill blood in a holy place?"

"This was not my doing. Lisandro brought you here. Though, looking at the high walls and fortified gate, I can understand why. I don't wish to kill anyone but if it comes to it, I will," he replied.

Diego sent one of his men to the top of the bell tower to keep watch on the road which led in from Villabona. Unless Perez and his cronies decided to come over the high mountain, this was the only way in to Irura.

While they waited, Maria came and sat beside Diego in the courtyard. They linked hands and smiled at one another. Diego chuckled. "I can just imagine how it would have looked when the Duke of Tolosa came riding into Castle Villabona. We have to hope that no one decided to shoot him on sight."

Maria flinched and squeezed his hand hard. She couldn't bear to think about Lisandro being in danger. Not knowing where he was and what he was going through was sheer torture.

"You are genuinely worried about him, aren't you?" said Diego.

"I love him, Diego. I'm going to marry Lisandro de Aguirre."

He let go of her hand and turned her to face him. "I know I agreed with Lisandro that marriage might be a necessity if he managed to find you, but there are other ways we could fulfil our obligations to him. A large sack of coins might be enough of a reward for Don de Aguirre, rather than claiming your hand. And then Father could offer a hefty bride price to entice the Count of Bera to marry you."

Maria got to her feet. "You think I am going to marry Lisandro as a way of saying thank you? No. And it's not because I see him as some sort of hero either—notwithstanding the fact that he *is* a brave man. I am marrying Lisandro because we love each other, and we have made a commitment. I won't be marrying anyone else, let alone Juan Delgado."

Diego's eyes narrowed. "What do you mean 'a commitment?'"

She let silence be her answer. Diego let out a long, low series of curses, all of which would get him excommunicated if the abbess ever found out.

"Well, I don't expect Count Delgado Grandes is going to offer for you now anyway. He lost interest once you disappeared. If he discovers that you have been with Lisandro de Aguirre unchaperoned, that will be the end of it."

Maria didn't care if she never saw Don Delgado ever again. The man didn't care for her; he only wanted power.

A loud whistle from the bell tower put a hasty end to their discussion. The lookout signaled the number three with his fingers. He covered his face with his hands and shook his head from side to side.

What does that mean?

"Three men on the road. The Englishman with the scarred face is one of them," said Diego.

She nodded. Of course, that was what the last signal had meant. Lisandro had obviously mentioned Mister Wicker in his note to Diego.

"You had better go inside. If there is to be any fighting, I want it over and done with quickly. I am not having you injured or killed this close to home. Mamá would never forgive me."

Maria headed back upstairs to her vantage point. She wanted to see the man responsible for her kidnapping once more. To finally get a good look at him.

The gate of the convent slid open and Wicker and his men stepped inside. Diego's man appeared from behind a nearby tree and closed the entrance. A loud *clang* resounded through the courtyard. The rest of

Diego's guards boldly stepped out from their hiding places with pistols drawn and aimed at the new arrivals.

Within seconds, the two men accompanying Wicker had thrown down their swords and dropped to their knees, hands clasped while they begged for mercy.

"Cowards," spat Wicker.

Diego strode out the front door of the convent, pistol aimed directly at Wicker's head. "My English friend, you appear lost, or else why would you be at a Catholic convent?"

Maria held her breath.

"I am just visiting various churches in the region," replied Wicker. He shifted to one side, and Diego's pistol followed. The Englishman was clearly testing him. "Come on, lad, put that down. You don't want to be firing at a live target. You might hurt someone."

With that, Wicker lunged forward, making a sudden move for Diego's pistol.

There was a bang and a small cloud of smoke appeared. Wicker dropped to his knees before falling facedown onto the stones. His body gave a violent twitch and then stilled.

Maria put a hand to her mouth. The Englishman was dead.

The other men were quickly clamped in irons and led out the front gate. She hoped to never see either of them again. For ever after, Maria would never be able to understand why Wicker had done it. Had he been counting on her brother not having the courage to pull the trigger?

She hastened downstairs to where a clearly shaken Diego stood staring at the lifeless body of Wicker. Blood slowly seeped out from under his corpse, staining the ground red.

As she approached, their gazes met. Diego shook his head.

"You had no choice. It was either him or you," she said.

He sucked in a shaky breath. "Yes, I know. But I just killed a man, and that is going to take some time to absorb."

Maria placed a hand gently on her brother's arm. There would be a time and place for a comforting hug, but that was not now. "Let me get your horse, Diego. It's time we went home."

Chapter Thirty-One

There was an eerie silence as Diego led his men inside the central courtyard of Castle Villabona sometime later that afternoon. The last horse in the group had Wicker's body draped and tied over it.

Maria, who was seated behind her brother on his horse, sensed something terrible had happened.

Servants silently took a hold of the reins of the horse and Diego jumped down. He turned and lifted Maria, setting her onto the ground. She swayed unsteadily on her feet and accepted his arm as support.

I am home. But what have I come home to? Please lord let it not be bitter-sweet grief.

"There were times when I thought I would never see this place again," she whispered.

Diego blinked away tears. "As did we," he said, his voice breaking.

The peculiar hush followed them upstairs and into the main chamber. Where usually there was a host of servants and family gathered, there was just her father waiting.

At the sight of him, she dashed across the floor and into his embrace. Strong arms enveloped her and held on tight.

"My sweet daughter. Oh, Maria, I feared we had lost you," he said.

His hand stroked her hair as he rocked back and forth. From his lips came a prayer of thanks. *"Gracias, Dios, por todas tus bendiciones. Gracias. Gracias."*

She drew back, a sheen of tears blurring her vision. The worry of not knowing his daughter's fate was visibility etched in her father's face. He had aged years in the months since she had last seen him.

He smiled at her. "And to think we have the Duke of Tolosa to thank for your safe return."

Maria couldn't help herself any longer. "Where is Lisandro?"

His tepid smile grew wider. "Outside on the terrace with your mother. Last night, when we found out that you were still alive and close to home, she went to our private family chapel and took up an all-night vigil. It was the only place she felt she could go and stay away from Señor Perez."

Diego came to her side. "Mamá was worried that if she saw him, she wouldn't be able to control herself. She was all for running him through with a sword."

"After Don de Aguirre revealed where you were, Perez went straight to the Englishman and told him. You should have seen his face when upon his return, the guards seized him and threw him into the same cell that the Duke of Tolosa had so recently vacated," said her father.

Maria held her hands together. Lisandro had been right. He had baited the trap, and the traitorous Perez had walked straight into it. "I still find it hard to believe that he would betray us. What will happen to him?"

"He will receive justice. I will ask for the Holy Hermandad to intercede on my behalf. They will interrogate Perez and then put him on trial. If King Ferdinand is indeed behind your abduction, he will surely distance himself from such a heinous crime. I expect Perez will see out the last of his days in Puerta de Toledo prison."

Her heart went out to her father. To discover that his long-serving faithful servant had turned against him and betrayed the Elizondo family must have been devastating. Señor Perez had chosen money and power over loyalty.

She turned to Diego. For all his bravery, Diego still appeared badly shaken by what he had done. Taking the life of a man was no small matter.

"After what happened at the convent, perhaps you and Papá might need some time alone. I shall leave you and go to find Mamá."

Slow, purposeful steps marked her progress as Maria made her way out to the terrace. She wore a veneer of calm, but inside she was shaking.

The instant she stepped into the mid-afternoon sunshine and caught sight of her mother's beloved rose garden, long-suppressed emotions rose like a tidal wave and washed over her. With a keen born of heartache, Maria dropped to her knees, hugging herself tight. She wept unconsolably.

"Maria!"

There was a scurry of feet, and soon, arms enfolded her. Her senses were filled with the familiar scent of her mother's perfume. The notes of rose, orange blossom, and jasmine were all that she needed to finally know that she was truly home.

Home.

It took a long time to summon the strength to lift her head and gaze upon her mother's face. In those early dark days when she'd been in the hands of her kidnappers, the promise she had made to her mother had been Maria's rock. The thought of seeing her again had been her greatest source of hope.

"Mamá," she whispered, her voice breaking.

"*Mi niña hermosa.*"

Maria smiled. She might be a grown woman, but to her mother she would always be her beautiful girl.

"You made a promise to come back to your family. That promise is now fulfilled," said Lisandro.

Maria glanced up as he came to stand beside them. Her barely abated tears quickly started again. "Yes, and you were the one who helped bring me home."

Miracles were something she had been raised to believe in, and now she had several of her own. She was home, back with her family. And the man she loved was here.

"Mamá, I see you have met Lisandro," she said.

Her mother nodded. "Yes. Though I still cannot believe that it was the Duke of Tolosa who went all the way to England to rescue you."

Lisandro held out a hand and helped the duchess to stand. He then took a step back and grinned at Maria. "Do you require my assistance or is this another one of those moments when you tell me that you have been leaping to your feet since you were a child?" he teased.

Her mother's mouth opened on a small *O*, but Maria simply laughed.

"You are never going to allow me to forget that remark about the Andalusians, are you?" She accepted his outstretched hand, then fell into his arms as soon as she was upright. He didn't protest when she reached up and planted a soft kiss on his cheek. The sooner her family understood the true nature of her and Lisandro's relationship the better.

To her mother's questioning look, she nodded. "I have agreed to marry Lisandro."

A red-faced Lisandro cleared his throat. "I hadn't quite got to that part yet. I'd thought it better to wait until you and Diego had returned before broaching the subject."

She gifted him with a second kiss, this time on the lips. Little more than an hour ago, she had seen a man die; and after all she had been through, Maria was determined that life was for living. She wasn't going to waste another minute waiting to begin a new one as Lisandro's wife.

The duchess clasped her hands together. On her lips sat a small smile, but her eyes glinted with joy. "Well then, Don de Aguirre, may I suggest you go and speak to my husband. Because if you plan to ask for our daughter's hand in marriage, you might want to first do something about putting an end to the feud between our families."

Maria and Lisandro exchanged a smile. Hand in hand, they followed the duchess back into the castle. It was time to settle the long-standing argument which had begun over a pair of goats.

Chapter Thirty-Two

I t wasn't how he had ever imagined asking for a woman's hand in marriage but considering the kind of day it had already been, Lisandro decided he should just go along with things. Besides, it wasn't every day that a hundred-year feud came to an end.

I hope it is coming to an end.

Seated around the table in the Duke of Villabona's private suite were himself, Maria, the duke and duchess, and Diego. In front of them lay an aged piece of parchment.

He had never seen the document before, but he knew of its existence, and of what his forebears had agreed to when they'd signed it. An agreement they had then reneged upon.

The duke pointed to a line of scrawl. "You can see clearly that it was in the terms of the contract. A contract the Aguirre family failed to fulfil."

"Papá," said Maria.

"Well, it does," he replied.

Lisandro held up his hand. "If I may. Yes, the contract stipulates those terms. My understanding is that my great-great-grandfather, the Duke of Tolosa, took grievous offense at the Duke of Villabona making unwelcome advances to his wife. That was why the final part of the deal was not completed."

The duke snorted. "Yes, well I heard she was quite willing."

"Papá!" cried Maria.

Lisandro didn't respond to the insult to his family. He, too, had heard those rumors. But if they were ever going to get this feud settled, both parties would have to make concessions. It was ridiculous that things had ever been allowed to get to this stage in the first place. Two pigheaded great-great-grandsires had condemned their descendants to keeping up a pointless feud which could have so easily been resolved if they had been willing to put their stubborn prides aside all those long years ago.

"Don de Elizondo, would you care to offer up an apology for the behavior of your grandsire?" Lisandro said. He calmly met the duke's gaze.

"Will you fulfil the contract?"

A look passed between them—a silent agreement that this whole discussion meant more than just settling an old dispute. It was the establishment of a valuable and trusted friendship

The two of them would do what they could in order to make this part of Spain safe against the machinations of the king. Men like Lisandro and Antonio had to take a stand and stop Spain from spiraling into a bloody civil war.

"Yes. I will fulfil the contract. Today. And on this exact day every year," replied Lisandro.

"Well then, I offer my family's formal apology for any offense caused to the late Duchess of Tolosa and succeeding generations," announced the duke.

Lisandro rose and offered Antonio his hand. It was quickly accepted. The ancient feud was finally over. There were smiles all around the table.

Lisandro nodded toward Maria as he retook his seat. She beamed at him. "And now, Don de Elizondo, I wish to discuss the matter of requesting Maria's hand in marriage."

The smile disappeared from Antonio's face. "I beg your pardon?"

Maria maintained her own smile. Lisandro might have caught Antonio unawares, but that didn't mean he was going to back down.

"I asked for your daughter's hand in marriage. For her to become the Duchess of Tolosa. What better way to finally put the feud to rest than by uniting our two families?" replied Lisandro.

Antonio's gaze fell on Maria. "But what about Don Delgado Grandes? I thought you were set on marrying him."

Never. That was all your idea. I don't even like the man.

"Since the two of you couldn't come to terms on the betrothal and dowry, I don't think it likely that he is still interested in marrying me. Besides . . . I have been away from home for many weeks in the company of another man. You cannot offer full assurances to the count that I am still pure," she said.

Her mother gasped. Diego punched the table. But, to his credit, Lisandro didn't bat an eyelid.

While Antonio's face remained expressionless, Maria noted that his right hand was fisted so tight that the knuckles were all white. Violence was not out of the question.

"Is this what you want, Maria? I am sure Don de Aguirre would never call your honor into question if you declined his offer," replied the duke, his voice dark with menace.

"Yes, it is what I want. I have already accepted his proposal," she replied.

Maria lifted her hand from under the table and slipped on the emerald betrothal ring. "When I first saw Lisandro in London, I thought he was the villain who had kidnapped me. I did as you would expect from a dutiful daughter and struck him solidly in the face. It took time for me to come to trust him, but I did. And then I fell in love. Papá, this will be more of a marriage than anything I could have ever had with Don Delgado. I ask for your blessing."

Antonio glanced across at Lisandro. "Did she really hit you?"

Lisandro nodded. "Yes, and she made my nose bleed. My friends had to drag her away before she could strike me a second time."

"Good. Then you know that my daughter has a temper and won't be caged. She will demand of you an equal partnership in your union," replied Antonio.

"I have already agreed to that condition."

The Duke of Villabona sat, slowly shaking his head. "What a strange day. So many changes—some for the bad, but many for the good. Yes. You may marry my daughter."

With a loud whoop, Maria leapt to her feet and into Lisandro's embrace. It didn't matter that her parents and brother were still seated close by. She set her lips to his and gave him the kiss her heart demanded.

Chapter Thirty-Three

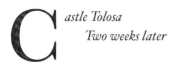 *astle Tolosa*
Two weeks later

"I swear I caught your father wiping a tear away during the service," said Lisandro.

He set two glasses of champagne down on a nearby table, then climbed into the oversized wooden bathtub to join her. Straddling him, Maria reached out and passed one of the saucer-shaped coupes to him before collecting her own.

Their glasses clinked together.

"He was quite emotional during the church service. It is not every day that a man gives his only daughter away in marriage," she replied.

The night before the wedding, Maria and Antonio had spent some quiet time together in his study. It had been her last evening as both an Elizondo and as a resident of Castle Villabona. Her father had gifted her several pieces of family jewelry, along with a letter.

The letter was one he had written, with the intention of sending it to the cathedral in Bilbao begging the kidnappers to spare Maria's life. She had barely read two paragraphs of it before breaking down. Every word spoke of a father's love—something that would never change, no matter where she was or by which name, she went.

Lisandro brushed a kiss on Maria's décolletage. "I must confess, I like your father. He is a good man. Which, considering that I was raised to hate him, is quite a transformation of opinion."

"I know for a fact he thinks you are rather special too. Both he and Diego hold you in high regard," she replied.

When the time was right, they would host their first family gathering at Castle Tolosa. All the Elizondo side of the family would be invited, along with the dowager Duchess of Tolosa.

But the next few days were for themselves. They were going to spend them alone in their private quarters, camped out on the enormous bed, sleeping, making love, then sleeping again. The only time anyone would see them was when the servants brought them food and more wine.

Lisandro took a sip of his champagne before setting it on a nearby table. Maria lay her head back as he took one of her nipples into his mouth. He slipped a hand below the water and between her legs.

"I am glad we decided to get this tub. I anticipate it will get plenty of use," he whispered.

She softly gasped as he began to stroke her sex. Her hand trembled, spilling some of the champagne.

He took the glass from her fingers and set it alongside his on the table. Maria rose up and then slowly sunk down, taking the full length of him. With her head settled in the crook of his neck, she proceeded to make sweet love to her husband.

"You know how I have always said I don't believe in coincidences?" he asked.

Maria gathered what remained of her thoughts. "Yes."

He thrust up into her. "I do, however, believe in fate. From that night when I first saw you, I knew you and I were meant to be together. That our futures were somehow entwined."

She lifted her head and stared into the face of the man who had saved her. The man she loved. "I was so disappointed when I discovered who you were. Angry at you— for being you. How could this handsome and divine man standing before me be my enemy?"

Their lips met in a tender kiss as their bodies worked together, reaching as one for that moment of shared ecstasy.

"I love you, Lisandro. And till the day I die, I shall always be grateful that you could see beyond that moment of my outrage and know that we shared one destiny."

That very evening, the *Night Wind* slipped quietly away from the Spanish coast and into the cover of the dark Cantabrian Sea. Its main deck was filled with the usual cargo of smuggled goods, all bound for England. In a sealed box, wrapped up to keep it safe from salt and water, was a handwoven Cuenca carpet—a special gift of thanks and love from Maria and Lisandro.

The address was marked on the outside of the box.

Master Toby Moore
C/- RR Coaching Company
82 Gracechurch Street
London, England

Epilogue

F*ive years later*
  Castle Villabona

"Go on." Maria handed the rope to her son and then pointed toward her father.

Young Esteban de Aguirre Elizondo looked with trepidation at the two goats which were tethered at the end of the lead before trying to offer the rope back to his mother. A ripple of laughter came from the guests standing to one side in the courtyard of Castle Villabona.

"You must do your duty and pay the debt," said Lisandro.

Esteban moved forward, one hesitant step after the other. To Maria's relief, the Duke of Villabona rose from his seat and went to greet his grandson. He knelt before the boy.

"What do you have there, Don Esteban?" asked Antonio.

The boy frowned. "The Duke of Tolosa b . . . bu . . ." He turned to his father.

Lisandro came over to his son and bent down beside him. "The Duke of Tolosa burdens me with the task of paying our annual debt.

These fine goats are to ensure that another year of peace exists between our families."

Esteban handed the rope to the Duke of Villabona, then stepped back and bowed. At least he had that part of the ceremony sorted.

Antonio clapped his hands with glee. "Such a wonderful sight. Two goats, my grandson, and my granddaughter. Oh—and my son-in-law."

A smiling Maria shook her head. The toddler in her arms squirmed and held out her hands to her father.

Lisandro got to his feet and took his fair-haired daughter into his embrace. "He is never going to forgive me, is he?"

After four, nearly five, years of marriage, the Duke of Villabona was still giving Lisandro gentle grief over having the temerity to rescue and then marry his daughter.

"You know secretly, he loves you. How could he not? You sailed all the way to England to save me, then came back and unmasked those who would destroy the Elizondo clan," she said.

If anyone was owed a goat or two, it was Lisandro, but the tradition had now become the perfect excuse for a big annual party. People from the surrounding villages gathered at Castle Villabona to mingle and celebrate as friends. Seeing all the happy faces was worth more than a thousand goats.

Maria lay her head against her husband's shoulder, her hand resting on her pregnant belly. It was always good to visit Castle Villabona, but it was no longer her home. As the Duchess of Tolosa she led a busy life, raising children and supporting her husband.

Spain was going through a painful chapter in its history, and keeping the peace took much of Lisandro and Antonio's time. But it was worth it to build a future for their families and to keep their nation whole.

It seemed forever since that fateful day on the beach at Zarautz. She still woke some nights in a blind panic, but Lisandro was always there to calm her down. To let her know she was safe and loved.

Life with him was a blessing, and Maria would always be devoted to her Spanish duke.

***

Thank you for reading! I hope you loved Lisandro and Maria's story and the magical landscape of Spain.

The next book in the **London Lords** is
PROMISED TO THE SWEDISH PRINCE

A fake engagement with only one rule.
Don't fall in love.

Swedish Prince Christian Lind is a prince in name only. As the youngest son of a youngest son, there is no fancy castle or vast wealth awaiting him.

His country has become a side player in the grand politics of Europe, so in order to make his mark he journeys to the one place where it is all happening. London.

Christian's childhood friend, Countess Erika Jansson is based in the British capital helping her father who is attached to the Swedish envoy. Erika speaks perfect English, she knows all the right people, and most importantly she offers to help Christian with his plans to become an influential diplomat.

But as individuals the walls of society are set high against them, and they quickly discover that they will need to work together in order to succeed. They come up with a clever plan.

A fake engagement.

After an elegant betrothal ball, Christian and Erika quickly become the darlings of the London social scene.

But brief touches and heated glances soon have them both wondering if there is more to their relationship than just old friends helping one another

CLICK HERE TO READ PROMISED TO THE SWEDISH PRINCE

. . .

Turn the page to read the first chapter of Promised to the Swedish Prince.

Rockstar Romance meets Historical Romance
 Regency Rockstars
 When faced with a dangerous new rival, Regency London's hottest lead singer is forced to place his singing career in the hands of a sexy widow.
 DOWNLOAD REID FOR FREE

Join my Facebook group for exclusive giveaways and sneak peeks of future books.
 Sasha Cottman's Historical Romance Bookclub

Sign up for my newsletter and get your FREE BOOK !
 A Wild English Rose.

Promised to the Swedish Prince
Chapter One

Lake Mälaren, Sweden
January 1813

Erika's teeth clattered together as the sleigh hit hard at the bottom of the dip. Tears sprang to her eyes. She loosened her grip on the top rail and attempted to wipe them away. The sleigh bounced again. She fell forward, arms flailing. A strong arm reached across her body and pushed her firmly back.

"Stop messing about and hold on. The next one is going to be even harder."

She glanced over at Prince Christian, hoping to show him that she was not the least bit impressed with his driving, but his gaze was fixed firmly on the horses and the icy edge of the lake which lay ahead of them. If the next bump was going to be worse than what they had just hit, there was every chance they were going to crash.

"*Jag vinner!*" came a cry from behind them.

Her head turned and she gasped as a second sleigh sped into view and passed them at a ridiculous speed. She caught sight of the driver. It was Christian's older brother Gustav. He looked back and gave a taunting laugh.

What the devil is he doing? I thought Christian was the only madman out here on the ice.

Christian yelled, *"Dra åt helvete!"* He cracked his whip over the top of the horses. Erika tightened her grip on the side of the sleigh and began to pray.

O Lord God. Rule and govern our hearts and minds by your Holy Spirit.

The high-speed run over the ice had now turned into a fearsome race. Brother against brother. From the hard set of his jaw, it was patently clear that Christian was not going to spare either the horses, or the sleigh's occupants. He would never back down when it came to a challenge from Gustav.

We are going to die.

The sleigh flew up a short rise. A blur of elm trees rose as a towering wall in front of them. Prince Gustav swerved left.

Erika held her breath and braced against the seat. This was going to be a tight turn. Her heart was pounding at a furious rate in her chest. Fear and adrenaline coursed through her body.

They hit a second deadly patch of black ice and the back of the sleigh suddenly slid wildly out to the left. Christian gave a worried glance over his shoulder and Erika's heart sunk. If he was concerned about how things were going, they were in serious trouble. Perhaps now was the time for her to leap over the side and take her chances.

As he turned his head back toward the front, he grinned at her—manic excitement was plastered all over his face. "Having fun?" he asked.

The horses pulled the sleigh back into line, and they both zigzagged violently in their seats.

Erika mustered a painful smile. No. This could not in any way be construed as entertaining or amusing. What had happened to his offer of a nice, slow ride over the ice and snow? And of her secret hopes of being alone with Christian and having time for them to talk, and perhaps share a private moment?

His impetuous nature is what happened. Of course, something like this was bound to occur. What was I thinking?

"Oh yes. This is great fun. In fact, I haven't had this much excitement since I broke my arm when I was thirteen, and had to have it reset without laudanum," she replied.

A scowl appeared on his brow. Trust Christian to think that a highly dangerous and possibly deadly race across the frozen tundra would be something high on Erika's list of pleasant pursuits. "You did agree to take a ride with me," he said.

"Yes! A pleasant ride along the side of a frozen lake—not a mad dash to my death," she bit back.

"I promise you won't come to any harm. And once I have rid us of Gustav, we can take the sleigh down to the water's edge and rest the horses. I would like to talk to you in private before we head back to the palace."

She nodded. "Alright, but in the meantime could you try to be careful and not kill us both?"

Prince Gustav was still ahead of them, but the back of his sleigh was now sliding about on the ice. From the way he was wielding his whip, it was clear he was doing his utmost to regain control.

Erika chanced another look in Christian's direction. The hint of a smile threatened on his lips. Any moment now they were going to crash, but the lunatic was still looking for a way to overtake his brother.

With the wind whipping through his fair hair, he looked every inch the wild, untamed Viking. His strong arms held the reins under his command.

"Hold on tight. I am going to make this next turn at speed," said Christian.

"Oh, sweet lord," she muttered. So much for him being careful.

Erika would have made the sign of the holy cross if it hadn't meant letting go of the sleigh's top rail. She sent another silent prayer to heaven.

"Ya!" he cried, urging the horses on.

A large elm tree loomed into view and Christian turned the horses' heads to the left. They were going to go around it. She hoped.

Up ahead of them, Prince Gustav appeared to have brought his sleigh back under his control and had slowed into the turn. Tracking wide of the trees, he successfully avoided a ridge of sharp rock which jutted out of the ice.

Christian pulled hard on the reins and a loud thwack cracked through the air. One of the reins had broken and it flew out of his hand. "Herrejävlar!" cursed Christian.

They were headed straight for the rock. The sleigh raced at a punishing speed. At the exact moment Erika realized that they were going to crash, time slowed to a crawl. She saw everything in slow, sickening detail as the disaster unfurled around her.

She pushed her boots hard against the bottom of the front piece of the sleigh, while one hand gripped hard to the top rail. Her other hand searched for purchase on the edge of the seat.

"Erika!" Christian cried.

The horses leaped over the stone, but the front bar of the sleigh smashed headlong into it. When they hit, they went in hard. Erika's world descended into chaos.

She was thrown clear—her body cartwheeled through the air. There was a momentary glimpse of sky before her field of vision was flipped and filled with the white of ice and snow. The ground came at her in a furious rush.

This is going to hurt.

She landed with a sickening thud on the ice, her breath whooshing out of her lungs. Pain tore through her body.

Ooh, my god.

If she could have sucked in enough air, Erika would have screamed. Instead she lay on her back, stunned and winded on the hard ground. Every inch of her body was on fire. Even breathing was agony.

When she opened her eyes, her sight was filled with the grey snow clouds which hung overhead. The dark sky gave her a moment's pause.

Am I dead?

There was a scuffle of boots on the snow.

"Erika, dear lord, are you alright?"

A familiar face swam into view. Blue eyes full of concern stared down at her. Christian. He was such a divinely handsome man. If she had died, then at least she had gone to heaven.

"Please say something. Anything. Tell me where it hurts. What can I do?" he pleaded.

She sucked in a short breath, then took in another deeper one. Tears sprang to her eyes.

"I hurt everywhere. I think you might already have killed me, so I would suggest you have done more than enough," she replied.

Fingers raced all over her body. Touching, prodding, poking. She was peppered with a constant stream of "Does it hurt here?", followed by "Please don't die on me."

She suffered his attentions. "No. No. Ow!" she cried, batting his hand away.

He stopped. His gloved hand settled back gently on her left knee. "I think you might have broken something."

She winced in pain. "I think *you* are the one who did that—I was just the passenger. Well, I was until the moment I became a bird."

He mumbled something that might have been an apology, but she didn't quite catch it. He went back to touching and asking her where else things hurt.

"I can't see any other obvious injuries," he said finally.

As the shock began to subside, and only the pain in her left knee remained, Erika's head cleared. Her breathing slowly returned to something close to normal.

Christian kept running his hands up and down her arms. He pulled off her gloves and squeezed each of her fingers.

"None of them are broken," she reassured him.

Of all the many times I have wished for you to touch me, why did you have to wait until you had smashed me onto the ice?

He sat back on his haunches, shaking his head and muttering words indecipherable.

"Do you think you might be able to stand?" he finally asked.

He gave her the gloves, and she slipped them onto her fingers before moving to sitting upright. Christian held out his hands, and Erika slowly, gingerly got to her feet. As soon as she stood, he put his arms around her waist and held her.

"Can you put any weight on that leg?" he asked.

"I am not sure," she replied.

The second Erika put pressure on her left leg, pain shot up her thigh and into her hip. She cried out. "Ow!"

"It's definitely badly damaged it," he said.

The rumble of a sleigh over the ice and snow had them both looking back toward the trees. Prince Gustav rounded the turn and his sleigh drew to a halt a dozen or so feet away. He leapt down and came to them.

"What happened?" he demanded.

Christian shrugged. "I was trying to take my ride tight and close to the rocks before sliding up to the tree and gaining pace by using the sleigh as a sling stone, but one of my reins broke. Poor Erika here got thrown clear and landed heavily on the ice."

Gustav's face turned ashen. "Are you alright, Countess Erika?"

Erika managed a meek nod. She had known both princes since she was a child. They had climbed trees, skated over the frozen lakes, and eaten more sweet cinnamon rolls together than she could possibly count. But for some unknown reason Prince Gustav had always addressed her by her official title.

"I shall live. Thank you for asking, Gustav. I think I have badly damaged my knee. It is painful to stand and place any pressure on it," she replied.

Gustav shot his brother a look of great displeasure which Erika pretended not to see.

"Christian, you are an outrageous fool. You could have seriously injured Countess Erika—even killed her. Though I notice you seem to have managed to walk away unscathed."

Christian's shoulders slumped. Erika couldn't help the twinge of sympathy which panged in her heart. It was as if the two years in age which separated the siblings was an eon when it came to who was the sensible and reliable one. It was Gustav the wise, versus Christian the reckless.

"Well, you were the one who started the race. We were just out enjoying one last ride together," replied Christian.

His brother growled. "You were going too fast long before I caught up with you. Besides which, you shouldn't be alone with the countess. It isn't proper."

"It wasn't entirely his fault. The reins broke," said Erika.

Gustav huffed loudly. "Please don't make excuses for him." His eyes narrowed and he gifted her with a look which could only be described as pained annoyance. "Countess Erika, I must voice my disappointment at you having agreed to be alone with my brother and ride in his sleigh. I thought you, of all people, would know better."

He had no right to be telling her who she should be spending her time with, or where. The nerve of the man. "Thank you, Gustav, but I am a grown woman. I can make my own decisions."

She wished that for once Christian would stand up to his overbearing brother—Gustav had a thing about lecturing people. His younger sibling most of all.

Gustav stepped forward and, pushing Christian aside, he came and lifted Erika up. She winced as he held her firmly in his arms while he carried her away to his sleigh. "I shall save you from my buffoon of a brother. The sooner we get you back to the palace and have a physician examine you, the better."

Heaven help me.

Erika gritted her teeth. Prince Gustav had decided to take on the role of knight in shining armor and there was little she could do about it. He was an annoying man, but he was also right. She did need to get urgent medical attention and his was the only sleigh still in one piece. "Thank you, Gustav. A physician would be most useful."

Christian stood beside the remains of his vehicle, looking for all the world like a puppy which had just been kicked. "I am sorry, Erika. Gustav is right. I was being irresponsible. I hurt you."

She winced once more as Gustav placed her onto the bench of his sleigh. The pain in her knee as she bent her leg was excruciating. "It was an accident, Christian. Let's not linger out here debating the whys and wherefores. I need to get this leg looked at."

The throbbing agony of her left knee was steadily growing worse and as much as she wished it was, otherwise, there was every chance that it was badly damaged. She had to get back to Stockholm Palace and have it seen to before her father found out what had happened.

Because while Prince Gustav might well be angry with his brother, his calm rebuke would be nothing compared to what her father would likely say when he discovered his daughter had been injured.

Prince or not, Count Magnus Jansson would tear strips off Christian.

CLICK HERE TO READ PROMISED TO THE SWEDISH PRINCE

Also by Sasha Cottman

The Duke of Strathmore

Letter from a Rake print, audio, FREE EBOOK

An Unsuitable Match (ebook, print, and audio)

The Duke's Daughter (ebook, print, and audio)

A Scottish Duke for Christmas (ebook and print)

My Gentleman Spy (ebook, print, and audio)

Lord of Mischief (ebook, print, and audio)

The Ice Queen (ebook, print, and audio)

Two of a Kind (ebook, print, and audio)

Mistletoe and Kisses (ebook and print)

Regency Rockstars

Reid (ebook and print) FREE EBOOK

Owen (ebook and print)

Callum (ebook and print)

Kendal (ebook and print)

London Lords

Promised to the Swedish Prince (ebook and print)

An Italian Count for Christmas (ebook and print)

Devoted to the Spanish Duke (ebook and print)

Wedded to the Welsh Baron (ebook and print)

Rogues of the Road

About the Author

USA Today bestselling author Sasha Cottman was born in England, but raised in Australia. Having her heart in two places has created a love for travel, which at last count was to over 55 countries. A travel guide is always on her pile of new books to read.

Sasha's novels are set around the Regency period in England, Scotland, and Europe. Her books are centred on the themes of love, honour, and family. Please visit her website at www.sashacottman.com

Printed in Great Britain
by Amazon